"Witty, whip-smart, and winning, Gina Fattore's *Spinster Diaries* is a sheer delight. In her tale of an anxious TV writer who turns to the lessons gleaned from her favorite writer—eighteenth-century novelist Fanny Burney—to navigate a health scare and ensuing existential crisis, Fattore expertly carries us from droll humor to incisive cultural critique, from lively comedy to utter poignancy."

— MEGAN ABBOTT, bestselling author of
Dare Me and *You Will Know Me*

"An utter delight from start to finish, Gina Fattore's debut is one of those rarities—a comic novel that is actually laugh-out-loud funny. *The Spinster Diaries* is a heartfelt, hilarious, and addictively un-put-downable story of anxiety, ambition, and love (or learning to live without it) in twenty-first-century LA and eighteenth-century Britain."

— ADAM LANGER, author of *Crossing California*
and *The Thieves of Manhattan*

"So you have this book about a semi-alienated (okay almost completely alienated), perpetually unmarried Hollywood TV writer adrift in a world of LA lunacy and blondes in zillion-dollar shoes. Throw in the fact that she spends her idle moments obsessing about an eighteenth-century novelist whose heroines are actually a lot less interesting than she is. Throw in a brain tumor. Mix and splatter. What you have is a woman you root for who makes Bridget Jones seem like a boring cow and a book that makes you laugh and, well, not cry exactly, because she is resilient, decent as hell, and whip-smart, and it is such a special pleasure to watch her find her unique way of being in a world that doesn't deserve her. Sign me up for the Gina Fattore fan club. I adore her."

— GEORGE HODGMAN, author of *Bettyville*

"Wouldn't it be cool if 'Gina Fattore' was really the pseudonym I chose for my prose writing, and it was actually me who wrote this funny, emotional, expertly crafted novel, and it was me whose witty and original voice was so fresh and captivating? Well, a guy can dream."

— GREG DANIELS, co-creator of such hit TV shows as *The Office* and *Parks and Recreation*

"Gina Fattore writes like the voice of your best friend in your head—that ideal friend whose unflagging support, self-effacing humor, painful honesty, easy rhythm, and bravery in all things great and small you want to turn to in times of distress. This is a rare and tricky feat only accomplished by the wittiest of writers. She also gets Hollywood exactly right. She sweats the small stuff hilariously, and gracefully handles the big stuff like the witty adult in the room. And the rooms she's been in contain a serious shortage of adults. Like Carrie Fisher, Fattore is funny as hell and in love with words and curious things; she's the quiet voice at the dinner party that you realize is also the smartest and funniest right around the time dessert appears. Once I realized she wasn't going to write about me in *The Spinster Diaries*, I relaxed and really enjoyed it. But I then got disappointed that I wasn't being subjected to her kind and ruthless gaze. Maybe in the sequel."

— DAVID DUCHOVNY, actor and author of
Holy Cow and *Miss Subways*

"Gina Fattore's tale of a TV writer stuck in showbiz purgatory is authentic, hilarious, and heartbreaking. Fattore serves as our herald into the capricious world of LA's entertainment industry, introducing us to a few of its central tenets: GirlWorld, (where expensive shoes and juicy dating exploits are required passports), Journaling For Anxiety™ (necessary when you're dealing with extensive script rewrites—oh, and being diagnosed with a brain tumor), and one giant passion project, a miniseries about the real-life English writer Frances Burney. Part social commentary, part confessional, part history lesson, Fattore's book asks the big questions: Why are women who choose their own paths without partners labeled as "spinsters"? If your brain tumor is benign, can you wait until hiatus to have it removed? And why do things always seem to work out in Woody Allen movies? I wish my diary was this much fun to read. Fattore's writing shines brightly in this amazing debut."

— DEBBIE GRABER, author of
Kevin Kramer Starts on Monday

The
SPINSTER
DIARIES

GINA FATTORE

PROSPECT PARK BOOKS

Published by Prospect Park Books
2359 Lincoln Avenue
Altadena, CA 91001
www.prospectparkbooks.com

PROSPECT
·PARK·
BOOKS

Distributed by Consortium Book Sales & Distribution
www.cbsd.com

Library of Congress Cataloging-in-Publication Data

Names: Fattore, Gina, 1968- author.
Title: The spinster diaries : a novel / Gina Fattore.
Description: Altadena : Prospect Park Books, [2020]
Identifiers: LCCN 2019034477 (print) | LCCN 2019034478 (ebook) |
    ISBN 9781945551734 (paperback) | ISBN 9781945551741 (epub)
Subjects: LCSH: Television authorship--Fiction. | Self-actualization
    (Psychology) in women--Fiction. | Burney, Frances,-1828--Influence
    --Fiction. | GSAFD: Satire.
Classification: LCC PS3606.A853 S65 2020 (print) | LCC PS3606.
    A853 (ebook) | DDC 813/.6--dc23
LC record available at https://lccn.loc.gov/2019034477
LC ebook record available at https://lccn.loc.gov/2019034478

Cover design by Mimi Bark
Cover illustration by Sandra Chiu
Book layout and design by Amy Inouye, Future Studio

Printed in the United States of America

"I go on, occasionally, with my Tragedy. It does not much enliven, but it soothes me."

—FRANCES BURNEY,
letter to her sister, April 1790

FRIDAY, JANUARY 13, 2006

FOUND OUT TODAY that I have a brain tumor. Which was upsetting. But not nearly as upsetting as losing my car at the Beverly Center. You know that feeling, right? That totally lost feeling where you're wandering in circles around an unjust universe thinking...

> SELF (V.O.)
> But this is exactly where I left
> it.

It's clear you have a problem: no car. But on the sliding scale of human misery, how high does this really rate, this lost car at the Beverly Center? Higher than a hangnail, lower than a brain tumor. Or is it? The brain tumor, after all, is benign and—for the moment—seemingly asymptomatic, whereas the lost car....

The lost car is a logistical nightmare begging a wide variety of deep philosophical questions. How long should I look before I accept that it's gone? An hour? Two? And once I've crossed that bridge—once I've accepted the very real possibility that my silver Volkswagen Beetle convertible might actually have been stolen from the fourth floor of the Beverly Center while I was inside attempting to return an ill-fitting corduroy jacket to a Gap that no longer exists—whom exactly do I call? The police? My insurance company? A significant other? What if you have no significant other? What if you're wandering around the Beverly Center parking garage on Friday the 13th with a brain tumor, a lost car, and a bright-red corduroy jacket you never should have bought in the first place, when right then and there, in that exact instant, you have the should-be-life-changing realization that all the others in your life are, for the most part, largely insignificant? What then?

Keep looking?

Give up?

Put the bright-red corduroy jacket on for added warmth?

It's not like it does any good to panic in situations like these. Or, wait, maybe it does. Panicking *is* always an option—although it tends to play better on female leads who are younger than thirty-seven and thinner than a size fourteen. If nothing else, it's cathartic. Tears. A few sobs. Maybe that's what I need right now? A catharsis of some sort? In a Hollywood romantic comedy like the one I'm currently trying to write, panicking would totally do the trick and might even attract the attention of a blandly handsome, age-appropriate single guy, thereby leading directly to eighty-eight minutes of banter and some kind of real estate–based happy ending.

Yes, that could totally work.

In a romantic comedy, the scene where the heroine wanders around the Beverly Center parking garage in a desperate search for her lost car could wind up being the Meet Cute.

Or the Point of No Return.

Or possibly even the Climactic Moment of Character Growth.

Here is what happens in real life...

A little old lady barely tall enough to see over the steering wheel of the car she only takes out on weekends slows to a crawl, rolls down her window, and shouts to me across the chasm of her empty passenger seat...

```
          LITTLE OLD LADY
    Oh, honey, did you lose your
    car?
```

Pity. From the elderly. I suppose that's as good a place to start as any.

Okay, false alarm. It was on the third floor. Not the fourth. Crisis averted. Now that I'm safely tucked back home in the Miracle Mile, I can see that going to the nearest available mall wasn't necessarily the best way to cope with bizarre, anxiety-producing medical news. Call a friend? That's something people do, right? I have some friends, sure, but if I were to call one of them and tell them I have a brain tumor, I'm not exactly sure how that would help the situation. I mean, once I got past the part where the tumor is benign (*it's not really a brain*

tumor; I'm going to be fine etc. etc.), then I'd just be stuck making small talk about meetings both canceled and taken and creating vague plans to get together that will never be fulfilled because, you know...*traffic, work.*

No, I think the important thing right now is just to remain calm. Remaining calm has always worked super well for me in the past. Because, really, let's get serious here for a second. My situation? Not that dire. True, I am a single, unemployed, thirty-seven-year-old television writer with a tiny little brain tumor pressing on my frontal lobe. But, again, it's not like I have cancer or an actual disease or anything—that's in the pro column. And being unemployed is pretty normal for a TV writer. We're all unemployed *some* of the time—like landscapers in cold climates. Being single...pro or con? I'm not really sure. I'm one of those dyed-in-the-wool perennially single types who's never been any other way *except* single, so I have no basis for comparison. Married ladies, is it better over there on the other side? Fancy dishes? Tax breaks? Is all that stuff helpful when you have a brain tumor, or does it just create a lot of extra domestic chores you have to deal with?

That romantic comedy screenplay I just started writing? That's definitely in the pro column. If I play my cards right, it could help me rocket my career to the next level—where I suddenly become A-list, get invited to tons of cool parties, and start hanging out with famous people. As opposed to the level I'm at now, where

I'm either making good money working on a show that is about to be canceled, or making no money developing my own ridiculously impractical ideas that are set in the eighteenth century. At the moment, I've got three whole pages of my new screenplay written, and I have to say I'm very excited about all three of them.

Or, you know, at least the first two.

The pages I wrote *before* my ridiculously suave, Omar Sharif–like ear, nose, and throat doctor called and told me I have a small brain tumor pressing on my frontal lobe? Those two definitely rock. They're clear, concise, funny—totally *not* set in the eighteenth century—and completely consistent with all the rules set forth in *Rules for Romantic Comedy*, the trusty how-to-write-a-screenplay book I just picked up at the Beverly Center, along with *Journaling for Anxiety™* and *Dress Your Family in Corduroy and Denim* by David Sedaris. Seriously, who can resist those buy-two-get-one-free stickers? Margaret Hale Newman, PhD, is the author of this trusty screenwriting guide, and although I've never met her, heard of her, or read any screenplays she's written, based on the parts I skimmed while standing in the aisle at Borders, I feel like the two of us are going to get along just fine. Without even trying, I seem to have fulfilled her first and biggest commandment:

Establish a sympathetic, likable heroine and her everyday life.

Check. I've totally done that with my heroine.

She's a middle-school teacher in the Chicago suburbs who wears baggy sweaters constantly—you know, sorta like Sandra Bullock in *While You Were Sleeping*, except really, she's based on my friend Kitten. Screenplay-wise, I'm definitely off to a good start—no question about that—but in dealing with my health crisis, I seem to have floundered. They're really not calling me back, are they? The brain surgeon's office? While I was wandering around lost at the Beverly Center, it seemed totally possible that they might call me back, that I'd be able to build a little forward momentum, set up an appointment or something, but now it's after 6 on Friday, and—oh shit.

Shit, shit, shit.

I just realized something...*three-day weekend.*

Martin Luther King Day.

Ugh. Now it's pointless to hope, right? No way is any sort of trained medical professional calling me back before Tuesday at 9 a.m. Till then it's just me and Google, doing our best not to panic, fear the worst, have negative thoughts, contemplate our mortality, etc. Thankfully, if you Google "meningioma"—the tumor-substitute word my ridiculously suave ENT kept using on the phone earlier today—the word "benign" comes up a lot. Benign means good. Gracious. Kindly. Or, according to the OED online, when specifically related to diseases, "Of a mild type, not malignant."

Mild. What I've got here is a mild case of brain

tumor. And the more I think about it, there's no possible way this can end badly, because the whole thing began—only three short weeks ago—almost exactly like *Hannah and Her Sisters*. I can't tell you how much this bathes me in relief. My tumor—like my screenplay—has a genre. And that genre is romantic comedy.

TUESDAY, FEBRUARY 14, 2006

IT IS A TRUTH universally acknowledged that no one really wants to be at the brain surgeon's on Valentine's Day.

Especially not someone who's currently Journaling for Anxiety™ and using her bipolar, heroin-addicted high school friend Hildy as her emergency contact person.

I should probably change that to one of my hyper-responsible sisters in the Midwest, right? That would make more sense. But doesn't it have to be someone who lives nearby? Isn't that how emergency contact people work? Obviously, forms like these are what make getting married seem so appealing. I have to say, it's never really occurred to me as a life option, but maybe I need to set my bar higher. Aspire to bigger things? Growing up, I really only had two dreams for myself, two things I absolutely, positively needed to accomplish: I wanted to be a writer and I wanted to not live with my parents.

If you count TV writing as writing, I managed to achieve both those goals before I hit thirty, and since then I've been resting on my laurels, dream-wise. Everyone else I know seems to be going full stride for the Having It All thing: two cars, two kids, rewarding careers, affordable cashmere, a great sex life, hiking trips to Bhutan. Can someone please explain to me how a generation raised on Morrissey and the omnipresent threat of nuclear annihilation found the gumption to attempt all that in their midthirties? Me, I'm mostly good with what I've got:

A great job as an unemployed TV writer.

An agent who calls me back.

A newfound ability to fit into the so-called normal sizes.

At this stage, asking for more just seems... well, presumptuous. Blasphemous, even. Like I'd be tempting fate, which probably isn't the safest way to kill time while you're waiting to get a second opinion from one of LA's most prestigious brain surgeons.

The first brain surgeon I saw wasn't just a brain surgeon. He was also the brain-surgery consultant for a one-hour drama pilot about a gruff-but-lovable brain surgeon who's great at his job but has horrendous interpersonal skills. His pilot got shot last year but didn't make it on the fall schedule, which is no reflection, of course, on the quality of the writing, the acting, the directing, or the brain-surgery consulting. It's just how things work in TV. Failure is our copilot; it's something we're all used to. I mean, so what if this particular brain surgeon wiped out last pilot season and failed to get a show on the air? Heck, the pilot I wrote last year didn't even get shot, so if we're keeping score (which we are, I mean, *hello*, this is LA), the brain surgeon's TV career is going way better than mine. Plus, he's got the whole brain-surgery thing to fall back on. I actually liked him a lot, Brain Surgeon #1. Casting-wise, he was older than I am but not too old—like maybe fiftyish—and much to my delight, he was gloriously, refreshingly blasé about the prospect of drilling into my head and taking something out. He played the situation like it was super low-stakes, which is exactly how I tried to explain it the other day to my bitchy, control-freak older sister—you know, the Hannah of my own personal *Hannah and Her Sisters*—but she got all stressed-out and confused and missed her exit on the expressway, so obviously I wasn't explaining it correctly.

Yes, I have a brain tumor—a subfrontal midline meningioma, to be exact. But it's kind of more like a mole. A sort of *internal* mole. *Maybe* it's compressing my olfactory nerve and significantly decreasing my sense of smell. *Maybe* it explains why I get so many headaches. Or maybe my sense of smell is just fine—coffee, anyone?—and constant headaches are par for the course when you're addicted to caffeine and ninety percent of your job consists of responding politely to rude criticism from showrunners, studio execs, network execs, and actors with suspiciously large heads.

According to Brain Surgeon #1, I've basically got two choices here:

1) Have brain tumor taken out ASAP at a total cost to me of only one eyebrow.

2) Ignore brain tumor, pretend it's not there, focus on other things, continue working on romantic comedy screenplay, etc.

Option #2 is definitely covered by insurance. Plus, it's less invasive. In medicalese, they call this "watch and wait." If I go with Option #2, I will have to come back in six months for another MRI, but until then I'm officially off the hook. In both scenarios, I get to keep my hair, which is a huge relief to me because, in all honesty, my hair is the only thing I've ever really liked about myself. It's got this sorta vaguely Pre-Raphaelite thing going on, and from the right angle on a supergood-hair day, it might look a little like Helena Bonham Carter's in *A Room with a View*. Not a *lot* like Helena Bonham Carter's in *A Room with a View* because, let's face it, she's Helena Bonham Carter, and no matter what movie she's in, her curls—every time we see them—have just been meticulously arranged by a licensed hair care professional standing just off-screen with a large canvas bag full of styling products. Still, it's always been a source of pride to me, my hair—along with my ability to form cogent sentences and my Phi Beta Kappa key—and if everything the first brain surgeon told me is true, there will be no Sophie's choice.

I'll get to keep both hair *and* brain.

With only the slight possibility of a tiny scar on my forehead.

And the slim chance that I'll completely lose my sense of smell.

But whatever happens, the ball's in my court. It's all up to me: the proper care and treatment of my brain tumor. It's completely my choice. Apparently, this is the latest thing in medicine—this personal autonomy, this letting the patients decide things for themselves—and, me, personally? I'm not so sure I'm on board with it. I mean, it's not like this kind of self-rule generally works out so well in other fields of human endeavor. It's like when you let people make their own sundaes—the resulting sundae is generally lopsided, no? With far too many toppings. Or when you allow the actors on a popular TV show to decide which lines they will and will not say.

Or which of the other actors they're willing to work with.

Or when, where, and how they're willing to lose their on-screen virginity.

No, people have areas of specialization for a reason. Brain surgery. Teenage melodrama. Sundae-making. And when all is said and done, I can't help but feel that certain potentially life-changing medical decisions are better left in the hands of licensed, board-certified physicians and not delegated to, say, card-carrying members of the Television Academy.

But still, overall, I think, good news from the first brain surgeon. And the second?

Well, if the first brain surgeon's office felt more like a high-end boutique (like the kind of place you'd have to be told about by a chic friend who's super in-the-know about brain surgeons), the second, an "institute" at one of LA's classiest hospitals, feels more like—well, Loehmann's, I guess. You know, with the communal changing rooms. Or maybe Gate 77 at LAX. My appointment was for 1:30 p.m., it's nearly 4 now, and although I did have the presence of mind to bring a book—a great book, a true classic—quite honestly, I'm starting to lose it. Under normal circumstances, the wait would be fine. Really, it would—I'm not the kind of person who says rude things to the guy behind the deli counter at Ralph's when it takes forever to get a half pound of turkey, thinly sliced. So, in theory, I'm willing to give one of LA's most prominent brain surgeons at least that much slack.

Except it's Valentine's Day, I forgot my iPod, and with each passing hour I'm finding it harder and harder to concentrate on *Mansfield Park*.

Seriously. If Fanny Price doesn't stop going on about that fucking amber cross of hers, I may have to kill myself. Could the stakes in this book be any lower? I mean, you're invited to a party, and you're a poor relation so you're probably not the sharpest dresser to begin with, but this much angst over a necklace? People are dying here. Not me, of course. *I'm* not dying. At least not according to that first brain surgeon. But what about the rest of these poor souls—my fellow passengers here at Gate 77? Who's to say what's wrong with them? Maybe their brain tumors are not so benign. Or maybe they're tucked away like plaque in difficult, hard-to-reach places. Mine's right between my eyes, thank you very much. That older couple, over near the water cooler? Which one of them is sick? That agenty-looking guy, in the suit, with the Blackberry—no, wait, scratch that. He's obviously here with his mother. But check out the young Hispanic couple with the twins. Twins, people! Twins, as in babies. Little tiny babies at the brain surgeon's. One of them is wailing his head off, and yes, the crying baby does tend to contribute to the overall Gate 77 feel of the place, but, hey, can you blame him? *Babies* of any size and shape should not be at the brain surgeon's. Never. Ever. Under any circumstances. And neither, for that matter, should *Mansfield Park*, which—forgive me, Jane—lacks the sort of *Emma*-like sparkle you want with you when you're a mentally unhinged single girl all alone at the brain surgeon's on Valentine's Day.

Oh, thank god. That's me. They're calling my name. It's my turn.

FRIDAY, MARCH 17, 2006

THERE IS A CERTAIN kind of heroine who desperately wants her life to be like a Woody Allen movie when in reality it's probably more like *My Big Fat Greek Wedding*, and really she should just accept this, move on, and stop trying to pass for Jewish.

But this time my life really *is* like a Woody Allen movie.

I can confirm this because last night I actually re-watched *Hannah and Her Sisters* for the 80,000th time, outlined its entire structure, and wrote down all the most important beats and key turning points of the story. The beginning is about Hannah and her sisters (*duh*), but after that we meet Mickey Sachs, a stressed-out, overworked TV writer who's constantly running to doctors at the drop of a hat. Kvetching about dizziness and possible hearing loss, Mickey goes to see a distinguished, white-haired ENT who forces him to take a lot of tests that require him to wear silly-looking headphones. When those tests prove inconclusive, he goes for a brain scan, and then another doctor—this one distinctly less avuncular and distinguished—tells him that the tumor is inoperable and he's going to die.

Except that turns out to be a brief, fake-out fantasy sequence.

So really the whole "brain tumor" thing turns out to be nothing.

Or, not exactly nothing.

More like the launching pad to a really great second act.

The stressed-out, overworked TV writer quits his job.

He has a crisis of faith.

He regains his faith.

He falls in love.

Sounds good, right? Like it might be funny, but at the same time spiritually uplifting. With a great soundtrack and great New York apartments and actresses who wear their hair naturally frizzy because believe it or not, people actually walked around looking like that circa 1986. True, it's not considered canonical like *Manhattan* and *Annie Hall*, but *Hannah and Her Sisters* won not one, not two, but three Oscars.

Including Best Screenplay.

Which is probably why it exists as a book, an actual book, that you can buy and study if you are so inclined. You know, the way religious people study the Bible. They turn to it for advice and wisdom in times of stress, which is what I'm doing with *Hannah and Her Sisters* in the sincere hope that my brain tumor story—a story that begins almost *exactly* like *Hannah and Her Sisters*—will follow all the preordained, from-on-high rules for romantic comedy and end just exactly like *Hannah and Her Sisters*.

On Thanksgiving.

With two people in love and about to have a baby.

But how likely is that, really? For starters, the protagonist in my brain tumor story doesn't even have an overpaid TV-writing job to quit. That's right...*still* unemployed. Luckily, my agent, Arnie Greenblatt, is working overtime to correct this problem. Rumor is they might be hiring over at America's top new medical drama. You know, the one where all the beautiful people discuss their love lives over gaping surgical incisions.

In the second place—and this is perhaps the larger obstacle—I'm not the best heroine for a romantic comedy. In a pinch, I could be a best friend. But even that is a bit of a stretch. If we're looking to generalize, I think we can safely say that as long as I continue living and working in contemporary, twenty-first-century Los Angeles, no straight guy's ever going to catch sight of me across a crowded room and think anything but...

> HYPOTHETICAL LA STRAIGHT GUY
> Man, I wish that chubby writer-girl would move so I could get a better look at her petite-but-titsy actress friend.

But I'm not *deformed* in any way. I'm not like, say, four hundred pounds with thin, stringy hair, oversize Sophia Loren glasses, and a pathological fear of leaving the house.

I mean, yes, I am enormous. But here in LA the

concept of "enormous" begins around size ten, which is the point at which salesgirls in trendy boutiques begin to greet you with the phrase…

SUPER-SKINNY SALESGIRL
We also have things in larger sizes.

The sad, pathetic truth about me is that I've never really had the gumption to give "romance," in all its traditional forms, the old college try. Perhaps that's just sour grapes? Not valuing something you can't possibly have? There was a point—and this must have been junior high, otherwise what else is junior high for?—where the job requirements for romantic heroine were explained to me in exhaustive detail. A lot of work would have to be done in order for me to qualify. Losing weight was job one, but after that came make-up, bleaching, waxing, eyebrows, skin care, cellulite removal, and a not insignificant amount of personality revision. Even the normal-size, normal-looking girls were doing all this stuff, and there didn't seem to be an end in sight. Where they got the energy for it all, I have no idea. Later—much later, sometime in the early aughts—it would be explained to me that they all *liked* it, that the GirlWorld 24/7 Prettiness Struggle wasn't a job or an obligation. It was something women did for themselves—*for fun*. For their own amusement. At the time, I guess I didn't get that. To me, it looked like it was, you know...*an actual real struggle*. Something that was causing everybody a lot of pain and mental anguish. So when the choice was put before me, I just opted out and chose not to play. It's not like I haven't had my chances with men. No, wait. It is. It *is* like I haven't had my chances. Or else (and I suppose this is the more likely scenario), I had them and just never *noticed* that I had them. Which is sadder: to go through life and never find the person who's right for you? Or never to have bothered looking in the first place? Here's one thing I do know: I know it takes a very bizarre combination of megalomania and incredibly low self-esteem to believe—really and truly believe, with every fiber of your being—that you are the one person on the planet *for whom there is no one*.

And it probably doesn't help that my heroes have always been spinsters.

That's right. *Spinsters*. Everyone thinks we don't have those anymore, that they've disappeared from the face of the earth along with governesses and embroidered screens. But that's wrong. We do have them. We totally have them. We just don't talk about them anymore because it wigs people out to think of someone being a spinster and not devoting every second of her waking life to romance. No, in the present day, *relationships* are what make you healthy and sound and normal, and it's not enough to just *have* these relationships. If you're female, you also have to talk about them ad infinitum at book clubs and baby showers. And if you don't have them—if you, say, haven't been on a date since the first Clinton administration and love interests don't effortlessly drop at your feet whenever you happen to be lost in a parking garage—well, people basically equate this with being, like, a serial killer or mentally ill or something. I can't pinpoint exactly when this cultural shift happened, but we now live in a world in which it's decidedly more shameful for a woman to admit that she has *not* spent her formative years pole dancing for fitness, perfecting her blow job skills, and dressing up in designer clothes, than for her to admit that she has.

And I suppose that's progress.

Of a sort.

But the world wasn't always like this.

Take the young Miss Frances Burney, for instance. One of the great heroes of my life; one of the top five people I turn to for wisdom and inspiration in times of stress.

Never heard of her? Not surprising.

Frances Burney isn't Jane Austen, with her face all over coffee mugs and tote bags.

She isn't George Eliot—boring as shit but deemed to be important by the powers that be.

She's not in the be-blond-and-pretty-and-kill-yourself club with Sylvia Plath.

Or the be-hyperintellectual-and-kill-yourself club with Virginia Woolf.

But in her time, there was no female writer more famous than the young Miss Frances Burney, spinster, of the parish of St. Martin's in the Fields.

She was only twenty-six when her first novel came out—the unfortunately titled *Evelina, or The History of a Young Lady's Entrance into the World*. And what exactly does this young lady do? She comes to the big city for the first time, buys some new clothes, and gets swarmed by Love Interests both true and faux.

In other words, Fanny's first novel wasn't *just* a novel. It was a chick-lit novel.

One might even dare to call it a rather derivative, uninspired example of the genre—except that Fanny's first novel essentially *invented* the genre. You know, the one where a young lady buys some new clothes, has multiple Love Interests, and ultimately has to make some really big *decision* about her life.

When this strange new kind of book first came out, circa 1778, reviews were good, sales were even better, and since it was published anonymously, all of London was scrambling to find out who'd written such an entertaining little romp. Once the mystery was solved—once everyone figured out that 1778's It novel had been written by the nearsighted, badly dressed daughter of the town's best-known piano teacher—Fanny got very famous, very quickly.

Approximately as famous, I would say, as a modern-day reality-TV star.

History does not record whether she changed her hairstyle, dropped ten pounds, and started frequenting the more exclusive boutiques on Robertson Boulevard, but we do know that in her midtwenties, Fanny suddenly became A-list, got invited to tons of cool parties, and met more than her fair share of famous people. True, she wasn't exactly knocking 'em dead in the boyfriend department, but by the careerist standards of twenty-first-century LA, she was doing pretty well for herself.

My agent Arnie Greenblatt would have been proud to represent her.

And she wasn't just a one-book wonder.

Right before her thirtieth birthday, at a time when Mozart had yet to crank out his greatest hits and people still walked around looking like Gainsborough paintings, Fanny published her second novel—a much-anticipated follow-up in which another beautiful if incredibly naïve young woman comes to the big city for the first time, buys some new clothes, and gets swarmed by Love Interests both true and faux.

Teeming with parties, socialites, new hats, degenerate gamblers, and languid metrosexuals, *Cecilia, or Memoirs of an Heiress* was twice as long as Fanny's first book, three times more complicated, and, much to everyone's surprise, an even bigger and more spectacular commercial success. Copies flew off the shelves. Fans pointed and stared at her when she went out to public places—or they pulled up a chair and gave her an earful on how the "mixed" (i.e., not so happy) ending of *Cecilia* could be improved and made happier. They stood up and made a fuss when she entered rooms. They routinely addressed her as "Evelina" or "Cecilia," which is sort of like the eighteenth-century equivalent of going up to Helen Fielding and calling her "Bridget." In October 1782, while she was in Brighton with her BFF Hester Thrale, Fanny wrote to her favorite sister, Susanna...

> *You would suppose me something dropt from the Skies. Even if Richardson or Fielding could rise from the Grave, I should bid fair for supplanting them in the* popular Eye, *for being a* fair female, *I am* accounted quelque chose extraordinaire.

And she was. She was something extraordinary.
We all have obsessions.
Subjects we can't let go of.
Stories we need to tell.
Or at least I thought we did.
As I creep further and further into my thirties and worry more and more about the brain tumor pressing on my frontal lobe, it's beginning to dawn on me that not everybody spends decades of their life angsting and obsessing on the career struggles and romantic difficulties of obscure eighteenth-century novelists.
Some people get married and have children.
They try harder to get staffed on long-running

medical shows.

They don't religiously devote all their weekends, vacations, and hiatuses to constructing an expensive, impractical, six-part miniseries about a nearsighted, badly dressed minor novelist. Yes, this miniseries would involve a lot of corsets and very wide skirts, but I, personally, do not think one tiny little six-part miniseries is too much to ask for the woman whom Virginia Woolf once called the Mother of English Fiction. That is why I have been working on mine so assiduously for the last six and a half years of my life, in between my actual paying jobs on teenage melodramas. And even when I try to take up more normal hobbies—like dating or knitting or writing romantic comedy screenplays—they never seem to take. What makes a person work so hard on an impossible, impractical task when the end result is almost certainly failure? Denial? Stubbornness?

Or possibly a tiny little brain tumor pressing on her right frontal lobe?

Two of LA's top brain surgeons swear this can't possibly be the case. For the record, Brain Surgeon #2 wound up saying the exact same thing as Brain Surgeon #1—only he made it sound much more like a *Cosmo* quiz…

When it comes to big decisions like buying a house or a car, you…
a) dive right in, the water's fine.

b) agonize and second-guess yourself.

Close friends describe you as...
    a) gutsy, confident—a real risk-taker.
    b) plodding, conservative—a nervous ninny.

The celebrity you most identify with is...
    a) Angelina Jolie.
    b) Condoleezza Rice.

You've just been diagnosed with a benign brain tumor. Your next move is to...
    a) ask to have it removed immediately.
    b) wait six months, have another MRI.

One thing both brain surgeons are in complete agreement about is that over time, if my tumor gets bigger, possible side effects might include visual problems (if it hits my optic nerve) and (bonus!) *personality changes*. I think I could probably use some of those. In fact, it's been suggested to me many, many times that it's my odd personality—and not my size-fourteen frame—that needs to change in order for me to leave my spinster past behind and start cleaning up in the boyfriend/Having It All department. But for the moment, my brain tumor is still way too small to save me any money on mental health services. It's currently measuring in at a svelte 1.4 cm, which means that the choice of what to do about it is mine, all mine, and according to this new spin supplied by the second brain surgeon, it should be an easy choice, one based purely on *what kind of person I am*. I'm playing fast and loose with the medical terminology here, but it seems a certain kind of person, when you tell her she has something inside her head that's not supposed to be there, will get all badass Angelina Jolie and demand to have it removed IMMEDIATELY at a total cost to her of only one eyebrow; while a second type will be all, like, no fucking way are you cutting my head open if you don't have to. This second type will tend to be a little more sedate, more conservative. Her brain-tumor gut reaction might be a little more like that of Mickey Sachs in *Hannah and Her Sisters*, who says, and I quote...

MICKEY'S VOICE-OVER
I don't want a brain operation!
Once they go into my skull,
I'll—I'll wind up like the guy
with the, with the wool cap who
delivers for the florist!

Of course, with a *Cosmo* quiz you usually get that all-important *third* choice of action. You know, the gutsy yet still professional move that makes your personality assessment come out halfway between brazen slut ("Pound another margarita and make out with the hottest guy at the party") and timid nonentity ("Slink home early and watch *America's Next Top Model*"). No such luck with brain surgeons. With them, there is no halfway. No messy gray areas to navigate. You're either all in or all out.

Spontaneous, decisive risk-taker or plodding conservative.

Angelina Jolie or Condoleezza Rice.

The second brain surgeon presented me with this personality test matter-of-factly, utterly devoid of judgment, and since his cool bedside manner didn't give me any indication of how he *wanted* me to answer (yes, I am that much of a people-pleaser), for one brief second, I was stumped.

And then it hit me.

Maybe he's right.

Maybe all that's really required here is a modicum of *self*-knowledge.

A moment of psychic certainty in which I, the patient, understand and admit, once and for all, exactly *what kind* of person I am.

The kind who gets the guy.

Or the kind who gets to run the State Department.

And when you put it that way, there's really only one choice the modern spinster can make. Obviously I will not be having brain surgery any time soon. Option #2 is the one for me. Problem solved! Decision made. We can now return to our regularly scheduled programming.

TUESDAY, MAY 16, 2006

IT'S WEEK THREE of the upfronts, I still don't have a job, and my agent has just informed me that I have an edginess problem. When I got this news, I was standing on the sidewalk in front of Off Vine, temporarily rent asunder from my niçoise salad, cell phone semi-attached to ear. His basic point was that I wouldn't be in this mess if only I had a new writing sample. By "mess," he doesn't mean self-service brain tumor, existential crisis, or impulsive decision to go to China this Saturday. He means, quite simply and definitively, week three of the upfronts and no job.

Getting me a job is like a sport to Arnie Greenblatt. Always has been ever since that immortal day—some ten years ago now—when securing his good favor raised me from the teeming ranks of struggling, put-upon Hollywood assistants to the slightly less-teeming ranks of struggling, put-upon Hollywood assistants *with agents*.

Trouble is I'm not exactly sure what sport we're playing here. Two-man bobsled perhaps? You know, where he's the guy in the front who steers the sled, and I'm the dead weight in the back providing the necessary ballast. Or maybe—considering how fucking hard it has become in recent years to get someone who lacks experience in the criminal justice system a job as a TV writer—the better analogy involves Christians and lions. Is that a sport? Feeding Christians to lions? If so, this same time every year, Arnie Greenblatt enters the arena and prepares to face the metaphorical lions on my behalf. Only this time, I've fucked up my end of the bargain by not providing him with a shiny new writing sample that is dark and, say it with me, *edgy*. Apparently, edgy is what works right now, and *that's* what I need to solve all my career problems.

Not a romantic comedy.

Not angst-ridden teenagers.

Not chicks talking about love.

Something shocking and borderline pornographic.

He's not wrong about this. A friend of mine just sold something shocking and borderline pornographic to a major cable network, so I can totally see where Arnie's coming from with this advice. But stories in which underage girls who aren't wearing any underwear throw themselves at self-loathing, middle-aged white guys do not come naturally to me, and while I understand and appreciate that these are *exactly* the kind of stories 99.9 percent of the straight-guy agents in this town most thoroughly enjoy reading and selling, I'm not sure I'm in the mood right now to try and make all *their* jobs easier by supplying them with one.

What with my brain tumor and all.

And in case you're thinking…

                    SELF (V.O.)
          Poor him! Poor Arnie Greenblatt!
          He doesn't know about the brain
          tumor.

Don't.

Arnie Greenblatt knows all about the brain tumor, because one day back in January when I was sitting around anxiously waiting for the brain surgeon to
call me back, the phone rang and it was not the brain
surgeon.

It was Arnie Greenblatt calling to tell me that one
of the less-cool cable networks wanted to offer me a
pilot deal.

Because that's the kind of career I have.

My face is not all over coffee mugs and tote bags
like Jane Austen, but periodically, less-cool cable networks will call me up and ask me if I'd like to adapt
some young adult novel into a television series. As a
rule, the main characters in these novels tend to be au
pairs or backup dancers, and you can be sure that if any
of these YA novels ever actually get adapted for television, the au pairs and the backup dancers will all be
played by ridiculously hot girls, and after eight straight
years as a working TV writer, the sad, painful truth
about me is that I just don't have anything left to say
about ridiculously hot girls.

I'm out.

I'm done.

I spent all of my early thirties writing about their dates and their Love Interests and their adventures, but I'm not one of their tribe—I'm part of the tribe that, you know, stays home all the time. So when Arnie Greenblatt called with this not-so-tempting offer, I did something terrible: *I used the brain tumor as an excuse.* That's bad, right? Bad karma. Or at the very least, bad career management. And the sad part was that I didn't even have to use the brain tumor as an excuse, because Arnie Greenblatt, bless his heart, didn't even necessarily want me to write the pilot for the less-cool cable network. He knows I'm not hurting for money right now—the spinster lifestyle is nothing if not cost-effective—so the guy's got bigger plans for me. Plans that involve the giant-size paychecks you get in network television, as opposed to the more petite paychecks you get in cable television, and while I genuinely appreciate his confidence in me and my long-term earning abilities, apparently what you need to execute that sort of plan is—yes, you guessed it—*edgier writing samples.*

Ones with profanity in them.

Or crime.

Or high concepts.

Or girls who aren't wearing underwear.

And I get that. I wasn't born yesterday. But if Arnie Greenblatt really wanted me, for the sake of my moribund career, to write something edgier than the traditional, by-the-numbers Hollywood romantic comedy I just turned in to him a couple weeks ago—the one I *specifically* told him back in January I was writing—well, then he really should have told me that back in January.

Or February.

Or March.

Or possibly April.

Such news would not have gone unappreciated (or unheeded, really) any time prior to week three of the upfronts, when deals are made at lightning pace, writing jobs are filling up quicker than slots in the Jolie-Pitt family, and it's too late for me to do a goddamn thing about my alleged "edginess" problem.

Even if I wanted to.

Which I don't.

But did I say this? No, I just caved. It's what I do, the caving. What I always do when confronted with a swaggering, stressed-out individual—agent, actor, soldier, spy—holding forth with great authority on what's wrong with my writing. I let them talk.

And talk.

And talk.

And then I thank them.

It's a little quality I like to call *being agreeable*. At least that's what they would have called it back in Fanny Burney's day, back in the good ol' eighteenth century.

Nowadays, I think you'll find most people call it

being a doormat.

Not everybody is like this, of course. Some people, when criticized, stand up for themselves. They get angry or self-righteous. They tell people to fuck off.

Or go fuck themselves.

Or go fuck their mother.

These are probably the same people, now that I think about it, who opt to get their brain tumors removed immediately upon discovery. Do not pass GO, do not collect $200. David Mamet, it suddenly occurs to me, would probably go that route. Perhaps he'd have them remove it right there in the waiting room, with a penknife and a bottle of rye for anesthesia.

What he would *not* do is fold like a cheap suit on the sidewalk in front of Off Vine. David Mamet wouldn't *apologize* to his agent for being a shitty, lazy, unmotivated writer and then march back into the restaurant and continue giving pointless advice about how to get ahead in the entertainment industry to a friend-of-a-friend wannabe-TV-writer-girl so low down on the TV-writing totem pole that she can only *dream* of one day having a big-time TV lit agent yell at her for not being edgy enough. David Mamet also wouldn't agree to take a meeting on a sexy nighttime soap where female law enforcement officials fight crime in white tank tops. Where do I go? Just tell me where to go, and I will show up there. Welcome to staffing season. It comes only once a year. And for that, we are eternally grateful.

I wasn't kidding before, about that China thing. I really am leaving Saturday on the midnight plane to Hong Kong, and from there I'm connecting to Chengdu, where the pandas are. It's never been a particular dream of mine to see the pandas, but for the past six months my old college friend Kitten has been living in some remote, yak-filled part of the Sichuan province with no running water and not much electricity, and periodically—whenever she gets electricity—she sends me these emails saying...

CONCERNED AND PERKY FRIEND
You should come to China!

And frankly, back in April, these emails from the Sichuan province tended to be a lot more cheerful and optimistic than the ones I was getting from Arnie Greenblatt. His read more like...

ARNIE GREENBLATT
There aren't a ton of jobs on returning shows for a character writer.

At least I finished my screenplay. It all worked out! They got together in the end, my main character and her annoying boss's son. I've really got to hand it to

Margaret Hale Newman and her *Rules for Romantic Comedy*—the woman knows her shit. Once I made it past the Devastating Setback/Point of No Return (Rule #20), it really was smooth sailing to the Climactic Moment of Character Growth (Rule #25), followed swiftly by the Happy Ending (Rule #2). Really. Seriously. I think the Happy Ending took me all of about two seconds to write. It came that naturally to me. For about a day, I just sat back and basked in the glory of it. Then I spent another day obsessing on punctuation and shipped the whole thing off to Arnie Greenblatt, who waited for the weekend to read it and wrote back, via Blackberry, in his signature terse style…

ARNIE GREENBLATT
Good screenplay.

That's it. Just those two little words. So now the waiting begins. The watching and waiting to see whether someone might actually want to *buy* my romantic comedy screenplay. Plus, the waiting to see whether I will get a job this staffing season. And the waiting I was already doing on my brain tumor. And you know what they say about the waiting—hardest part, etc., etc., &c.—so that's when jetting off to China to visit my dear friend Kitten started to seem like a good idea.

Although I should probably clarify that I'm not going to the yak-filled, no-electricity, no-running-water part—I'm going to the Four Seasons part. This is going to cost an insane amount of money, yes, but keep in mind that if you are a moderately successful TV writer who is larger than a size ten (even if you are, say, a size fourteen or sometimes a twelve), and you have no mortgage, no precocious children in private school, and no current or ex-wives to support, there is literally NOTHING in the entire city of Los Angeles for you to spend your money on *except* expensive trips to China.

Oh, sure, you could go out and *try* to spend your money. But in order to do that you would have to know where the rich people shop (hint—it is not Bloomingdale's), and then you would have to be brave enough to walk into those places and face the incredibly skinny salesgirls of LA, and even if you happened to have that kind of knowledge—and that kind of courage—probably nothing would fit you anyway, and so you would come home depressed and wanting to kill yourself.

Whereas municipal bonds flatter all body types.

Just ask Harold, my business manager.

Of course, the real danger here is not financial ruin.

No, the real danger of spending thousands of dollars on a high-end trip to China is that by taking any sort of vacation at all—expensive, inexpensive, with yaks or without—I run the risk of inadvertently changing the genre of my brain-tumor narrative from a frothy, delightful *Hannah and Her Sisters*–style rom-com into one of those *Eat Pray Love/Under the Tuscan Sun/Year in Provence* jobs. You know, one of those stories where a stressed-out, overworked heroine goes on vacation and ends up being "transformed" by the beauty and simplicity of a foreign culture incredibly similar to the one her grandparents went to a lot of trouble and inconvenience to flee circa 1920, and then because she is so quote-unquote transformed by this experience, she quits her job, has a crisis of faith, regains her faith, and falls in love.

But again, how likely is that? Sure, chick-lit novels and romantic comedies are *required* to end happily. It's one of the rules. Not just of modern-day, how-to-write-a-screenplay gurus like Margaret Hale Newman. But of Shakespeare. And Jane Austen. And probably some super old guys like Aristophanes. Frances Burney did, of course, try to break that rule with the famously "mixed" ending of *Cecilia*, but perhaps that's why she never entered the pantheon of the greats. As for me, I just don't see how my story could possibly work out that way due to my overwhelming lack of Love Interests.

Where do they come from, all these Love Interests women are always going on about at book clubs and baby showers? Internet dating? That's the answer, right? Lately I'm hearing a lot about something called JDate, but I'm not sure that would work for someone who's only *pretending* to be Jewish so that her life will seem more like a Woody Allen movie. Plus, then I would have to undergo some sort of Makeover Montage (Rule #9)—you know, lose the glasses, learn to wear makeup, invest in a little black dress. When I was young, guys with beards were always hanging around my Brooklyn apartment discussing Marxist theory and trying to sleep with my roommate. Every so often, around 3 in the morning, one of them would give up and try to sleep with me. But I always said no. In Chicago, in my midtwenties, there were a few mixtapes of suspicious intent, some earnest conversations about *My So-Called Life*. But in my late twenties, I moved to LA to try to get ahead in the entertainment industry, and I guess maybe that jinxed things for me. The worst part is that we have this hard-and-fast rule here in Hollywood about how all the very best writing is always based on *personal experience*, so now I have to work overtime, 24/7, to keep my lack of Love Interests on the down-low. I can't let on to anyone that I'm a thirty-seven-year-old modern-day spinster who's never actually *been* in love—because then it's totally possible I might never work again.

At least not in the genre better known as Chicks Talking about Love.

And no one wants that to happen.

Definitely not Arnie Greenblatt.

And probably not me.

No, I have spent the better part of a decade—twenty-seven to thirty-seven, the one most women spend trying to get married and have children—attempting to get ahead in the entertainment industry, and even though I'm not totally sure *why* I'm doing this (money, fame, a house in the hills, better wardrobe, better trim level on my Volkswagen, etc.), obviously, it would be a real shame to stop now that I've clawed my way to the middle. This I will concede: my way of getting ahead in the entertainment industry—the way where you just stay home, be a spinster, and write all the time—well, that way has become significantly less popular in recent years. It used to be fairly common. I mean think about it…

It worked for Jane Austen.

Emily Dickinson.

Not one, not two, but all *three* Brontë sisters.

These are all women who got ahead in the enter-tainment industry by following the centuries-old, tried-and-true, stay-home-and-be-a-spinster-and-write plan. Although, as the official LA spokesperson for this plan, I should probably disclose that, well, not every-body sticks with the plan. The late thirties is a popular time to step off, leave your spinster bona fides behind, and cross over to the other side with the *married people*. You know, kind of like Miranda on *Sex and the City*. Or Charlotte on *Sex and the City*. Or that other, more fa-mous Charlotte: Charlotte Brontë, the most bitter and longest-lived of the Brontë sisters. At thirty-eight, she bailed on the plan for a clergyman named Arthur Bell Nicholls who had been hanging around on the sidelines of her life for a decade seeming sort of vaguely into her, and even though most sources seem to agree that she didn't love him…sure enough, reader, in June 1854, she married him.

And then ten months later she died.

Which doesn't exactly count as living happily ever after in my book, so I stand behind the stay-home-and-be-a-spinster-and-write plan. It's especially good for women who don't like domestic chores, taking care of babies, etc., although I can see how, in the post–*Sex and the City* era, it's probably going to need a catchi-er marketing slogan. Even if you shorten it and call it "The Spinster Way," it still calls to mind middle parts, unfortunate fashion choices, and sacrificing things for your art. Plus, lest we forget, the cruelest, most awful fate in all of GirlWorld: *dying alone*.

That's the tragic fate that befell Frances Burney, star of my ill-fated, six-part miniseries. The poor wom-an died alone in Bath on January 6, 1840, having had the fortune/misfortune to outlive her age, her fame, the fashion for really tall hair, and virtually every single person she had ever known and loved over the course of her eighty-seven anxiety-ridden years on the planet. Of course, when I say she died alone, I don't mean *to-tally* alone. I think she had a few nieces with her at the end, but that's not exactly what anyone dreams of, is it? When people go on and on about true love and not dying alone and all that, they're not hoping to go out with some devoted nieces by their side.

Still, making it to eighty-seven isn't bad, is it?

Especially in the age before Advil and aspirin and anesthesia. Back then, a severe chill or a lurking fever could eighty-six you overnight, yet somehow Frances Burney—Mother of English Fiction, inventor of the chick-lit novel—defied the actuarial odds of her time. Good genes were undeniably a factor. Fanny's hip, cool, suspiciously young-looking musician father lived to be eighty-eight. Hetty—her older, more Hannah-like sister—checked out around eighty-three or eighty-four, which becomes an even bigger accomplishment if you factor in seven full-term pregnancies, countless "vile miscarriages," and the type of extreme money woes that invariably result from marrying a musician. But Fanny's favorite sister, Susanna—the one who loved to play the piano and spoke French really well—only made it to forty-four, and obviously good genes don't tell the whole story. No, I have a strange little pet theory about this….

I think Journaling for Anxiety™ helped.

True, she didn't own the Beginner's Guide or the Workbook, but from the time she was sixteen to her death at the ripe old age of eighty-seven, Frances Burney wrote down virtually *everything* that happened to her. Diaries, letters, you name it—the woman was constantly writing. Sure, she also wrote for money: novels, plays, the occasional pamphlet. A girl's gotta pay the rent. But throughout her life, Fanny consistently wrote down all her *private* thoughts with lots of dashes and exclamation points and weird eighteenth-century capitalizations and abbreviations, "etc., etc., &c."—and here's the part where having some devoted nieces does come in handy: *it all got saved.*

That's right. All of Fanny's eighteenth-century Journaling for Anxiety™ still exists out there in the world. A bunch of impoverished academics have taken on the official task of sorting it all out, and their best guesstimate is that it's going to take *decades* to produce some sort of official, unabridged version. Till then, devoted fans are forced to rely on the many *abridged* versions of Fanny's diaries currently in existence—like the little pink Everyman's Library edition I accidentally stumbled upon one lazy Saturday afternoon in the stacks of the Beverly Hills Public Library. At the time, I had just moved to LA from Chicago with two suitcases, half a *Seinfeld* spec, and a sincere desire to get ahead in the entertainment industry, so when I found Fanny's diary, I didn't see it as an irrelevant artifact of a bygone era. No, I simply thought to myself...

> STRUGGLING 20-SOMETHING
> ASSISTANT GIRL (V.O.)
> Here is someone else who has
> tried to get ahead in the
> entertainment industry. I wonder
> how things worked out for her.

And since that fateful day, Fanny has always been there by my side. You know, sorta like Virgil was for

Dante. He was a real person, Virgil, a real poet. Dante didn't just make him up for comedy purposes. He used him to represent something bigger, although it's been a long time since college and I can't remember exactly what. I mean, Virgil never had his own miniseries, but he's definitely made it onto busts and things, and I'm sure he's gotta be famous for something, whereas the young Miss Frances Burney?

Well, with Fanny, one might say her defining characteristic is her ever-present anxiety.

Her angsting.

Her obsessing.

Her second-guessing.

And obviously, I'm supergood at all that stuff, too, which must explain why I plucked her from centuries past to be my patron saint. After all, second-guessing is basically my forte. I can second-guess others if it's required, but mostly what I do is second-guess myself.

Like my decision to leave town Saturday on the midnight plane to Hong Kong even though it's staffing season and I don't have a job.

Or my decision not to have brain surgery.

Or my decision to choose an obscure, nearsighted, badly-dressed eighteenth-century novelist for the heroine of my six-part miniseries when obviously Jane Austen would have been a much better, more commercial choice.

Or maybe a sexy-dangerous George Sand-type with

some top-of-show name recognition.

But it's far too late to turn back, isn't it? Basically, now we're stuck together, me and Fanny, which is fine because I sincerely *believe* in Fanny as a heroine. True, no one has any idea who the fuck she is. That's a definite downside. But that's just the nature of the game here in LA. Fame is fleeting. People get a break. They have their moment. And then if they don't manage their careers properly—if they take the wrong part, or turn down the right part, or do the irresponsible thing and run off to China during staffing season—they disappear.

Like that Shelley poem about the guy in the desert.

Or like Fanny when she took that awful job working for the Queen.

Ugh. That job. I wouldn't wish that job on my worst enemy. My worst *Hollywood* enemy. Staffing season was obviously a bitch that year too. Sure, she kinda *had* to take that job because of how badly everything was going with that evil bastard of a clergyman George Owen Cambridge, aka King of the Wishy-Washy. Thirty-four was old back then—super old, actually, to be both unmarried *and* unemployed. You know, like I am. And the job *was* incredibly prestigious. Not to mention well paying, and super hard to get. It even had health care: smelling salts, blisters, "the bark," etc. But no vacation days, no weekends off—nothing to do while the King was going mad. Because, you know, back in 1786, it wasn't considered appropriate to start composing your celebrity-tell-all memoir while still on the celebrity payroll. And after five years of that super glamorous and important job, five years of waking up at 6 a.m. to help the Queen get dressed, five years of walking backward and answering to a bell, the young Miss Frances Burney wasn't so young anymore.

Or so famous.

She was more of a footnote.

A Where Are They Now who hadn't published a book in nearly ten years.

She plugged away at her day job, for sure. And to pass the time, Fanny wrote these crazy blank-verse tragedies. But by the time she was in her late thirties—you know, basically my age—she started developing weird inexplicable health problems. Back then they couldn't just throw you into an MRI tube and hope for the best. Nope, in Fanny's case, opium was prescribed. And "three glasses of wine in the day." But nothing worked. She just kept getting weaker and weaker. She lost weight, couldn't sleep, and by December 1790, she was wasting away and near death—not from a small brain tumor pressing on her frontal lobe but from some nonspecific "feverish illness." If you ask me, it was the piquet that nearly killed her. I'm not really sure what piquet is exactly, but obviously it is some card game that makes you want to kill yourself if you are a thirty-eight-year-old spinster who's been trapped in a castle for three and a half years with a mad King, a passive-aggressive Queen, and a tyrannical German boss with a funny accent.

Plus, getting jilted for Miss Gunning and her 10,000 pounds doesn't exactly *improve* your mental health. But I'm getting ahead of myself. Obviously, I should be packing for China right now and not obsessing like a crazy person on my ill-fated, six-part, *Masterpiece Theatre*–style miniseries chronicling the career struggles, financial woes, and romantic difficulties of Frances Burney, Mother of English Fiction. Clearly, traveling the world and socializing with others is what normal, non-spinster people do with their free time, so here I go.

Bon voyage.

Top Five Possible Brain Tumor Symptoms

- Tendency to stay home and write all the time

- Tendency to digress about spinsters

- Sudden and complete lack of interest in *The New York Times* Sunday Styles section

- Trouble spelling words that sound the same but are spelled differently, e.g., there/their/they're

- Total enjoyment of Ashton Kutcher/Amanda Peet romantic comedy, *A Lot Like Love*

WEDNESDAY, JUNE 21, 2006

THERE IS A CERTAIN kind of female TV writer who wears $500 shoes and sleeps with actors.

I am not that kind.

But apparently several of my new coworkers are.

That's right.

Coworkers.

That's what happened to me while I was on vacation in China: I got a job. I was transformed, if you will, from an unemployed person to an employed one, and the person I have to thank for this transformation is, of course...

Arnie Greenblatt.

Because the second Arnie Greenblatt started putting it out there that I was "unavailable" to meet with anyone next week about being a co–executive producer on their television show, the second he started telling people I was leaving town Saturday night on the midnight plane to Hong Kong—well, then something truly amazing happened. That's right. You guessed it.

Suddenly, everyone wanted to meet with me about being a co–executive producer on their television show.

They met me for breakfast.

They met me for lunch.

They met me in a wine bar late Saturday night.

They met me even though my writing samples don't have any profanity in them.

Or crime.

Or high concepts.

Or girls who aren't wearing any underwear.

This turn of events came as a huge surprise to me, although in truth it probably shouldn't have, since it was predicted many months earlier, with great specificity, by my friend Jay, who said, and I quote...

JAY
Go to China. It will make you
seem more interesting.

Et voilà. It did. Although it certainly didn't make me seem *as* interesting as the girls I work with who wear $500 shoes and sleep with actors. They are all in their early thirties, i.e., younger than me, and thinner, and obviously lousy with Love Interests like all good romantic comedy heroines should be. And here's the weird part...

They seem to be having a contest to see which one of them can go the longest without re-wearing the same pair of shoes. From the looks of these girls, it will be a battle to the death, this contest, and I am pleased to have a front-row seat. I think I'm going to learn a lot from this experience. After all, it's not every day that a poor excuse for a girl such as myself—a confirmed spinster whose most expensive pair of shoes cost $169—gets this close to the GirlWorld inner sanctum. You know, where everyone wears expensive shoes and sleeps with actors. I swear I am not making that part up. Costars. Guest stars. Special guest stars. They have a lot of goings-on with actors, these women, and the goings-on appear to be of some sort of social nature, which is truly baffling to me, since every conversation I have ever had with an actor has started with him saying...

                    ACTOR
        I can't say that line.

...and ended with me crying in my hotel room and having to stay up all night to do a rewrite.

The show I'm working on? You've heard of it. Don't pretend you haven't.

Unless you're still in your twenties and you work at an alternative newspaper. Then naturally you have to pretend you haven't heard of it, and I'm fine with that. That's cool. A thousand years ago, when I was in my twenties, I worked at an alternative newspaper, and back then I was always pretending I hadn't heard of things like *Friends* and *Mad About You* and *Everybody Loves Raymond*. So I understand where you're coming from, but it's a pretty big hit, this show. At least, with the residents of GirlWorld. They've taken a spark to it across the board: the young, the old, the New York liberal media elite, pro-life groups...*my mom*. Rarely in the history of filmed entertainment has one television show been able to reach out and touch such a broad spectrum of the GirlWorld viewing population—tickle their funny bones, touch them deep down in their heart of hearts—but can I let you in on a little secret?

I don't really care for it much.

But that's fine! It's not my job to *like* the TV show I'm working on. That's not required. No, my job is to look at it from a distance, analyze it in Aristotelian terms, and dissect the primal fantasies it conjures up for its audience, without actually participating in any of those fantasies myself. Doing this all day every day 10 to 7 requires a little something called *artistic detachment.* All the people who super-super love the show and post things about it on the internet and send coffee mugs and flowers to the writers? They *don't* have artistic detachment—but me, I've got it in spades. I think I've probably *always* had it, even before I became a professional TV writer and discovered there was a way to turn it into large sums of money. Here's a fun test: when you were a kid, spacing out in school, trying to fall asleep at night, did you daydream long, complicated scenes, complete with dialogue, and think to yourself...

                    SELF (V.O.)
          Wow! Wouldn't it be cool if
          something like that happened to
          me?

Or did you daydream long, complicated scenes, complete with dialogue, and think to yourself...

```
        SELF (V.O.)
Wow! Wouldn't it be cool if
something like that happened to
a much thinner, better-looking
version of me who also solved
crimes?
```

Anyone who's had thoughts like that second one is highly qualified to become a professional TV writer. Seriously. Trust me on this one. I have had some doings with the American network television system, and if your mind just naturally works that way, then you've got what it takes. Frankly, the rest is just word processing. You know, choosing the proper margins. And nowadays there are computer programs that do all that stuff automatically. Plus, assistants. We have a lot of those around here at the new job. In fact, a new one just started today. He's quiet and sort of studious-looking. I'm not really sure why he started late, but he's a guy, so that explains the quietness. Guys, as a general rule, don't bond with their brand-new coworkers by talking incessantly about shoes and divulging lots of intimate details about their Love Interests. No, in LA they tend to bond over things like sports or rock 'n' roll or how much money various movies made at the box office. And can I just say...

God bless them for that.

Not enough is said in praise of men and their complete and total lack of interest in broadcasting the picayune details of their love lives to their colleagues at work. It's like they have this quality, this...I don't know...this *distanced* quality, that allows them to make it through eight, nine, sometimes even ten hours at a stretch without talking in excessively minute detail about the dates they've been on, the dates they're going to go on, the clothes they wore on the dates, who paid for the dates, and the phone calls they've received (or more often, not received) in reference to the aforementioned dates. It's interesting to me, this quality. This emotional reticence. I admire it. And now that I have a brain tumor pressing on my frontal lobe *and* some sort of fibroid cyst on my left ovary, I'm going to need every ounce of it I can get.

Yes, it's true.

Stop the presses.

I have another medical problem.

Right after I started my new job and refrained from celebrating my thirty-eighth birthday, I went in for my annual gyno appointment, and instead of everything being fine—which everything usually tends to be when you are a thirty-eight-year-old spinster who has never had any sexually transmitted diseases or mucked about with birth control pills—instead, everything wasn't fine.

And I guess that's fine.

Nothing that a little more Journaling for Anxiety™

can't cure.

Or perhaps some opium and three glasses of wine in the day?

I'm sure it's fine, this new thing I've got, this new source of anxiety. I've already had the thoroughly invasive and humiliating ultrasound test they give you for this, and any day now I'm sure my Ivy League–educated gynecologist is going to call and give me the all-clear. Unfortunately, I'm not writing a frothy, delightful romantic comedy at the moment, so I've got nothing to distract me while I wait this one out. Maybe I should start something new? Open a Western front in the war against low-level medical anxiety? Maybe try to pitch a pilot? It's almost the Fourth of July, aka summer, or as we call it here in LA…*network development season.*

Sure, some people might find this second medical problem alarming.

People who hate driving to Beverly Hills and are true hypochondriacs.

You know, people like Mickey Sachs in *Hannah and Her Sisters.*

Me, I'm not worried.

Or maybe I am.

Just a tiny bit.

After all, this second diagnosis does seem to indicate that we have now veered away from the frothy, delightful romantic comedy terrain of *Hannah and Her Sisters* and wound up in the second act of a medical show. You know, the part when the doctors who are either sleeping with each other or have bad interpersonal skills meet up in one of their standing sets, and then one of them says...

RIDICUOUSLY GOOD-LOOKING
DOCTOR-GIRL
Wait, we missed something...the
patient also has THIS.

And that raises the stakes and spins the story off in some new direction, and shit—those medical shows never end well, do they?

At least not for the guest stars.

The series regulars, the actual doctors, are usually fine—but in this story, I'm definitely *not* the doctor. No, I'm the patient, so maybe it's finally time to panic. You know, call my lawyer, get my affairs in order, finish the only task that truly matters to me: my six-part miniseries documenting the career struggles, financial hardships, and romantic difficulties of Frances Burney, Mother of English Fiction. It wasn't just my birthday last week—it was also hers. I turned thirty-eight, which now puts me officially in my late thirties. She turned...254. That's sort of funny, right? That we're both Geminis. Unlike me, the young Miss Frances Burney wasn't doomed from the start to wind up a thirty-eight-year-old spinster. She *chose* to be one. The girl had options. Or at least one option. The historical record is very clear on this point: When she was twenty-two, about to turn twenty-three, a short, sensible guy named Thomas Barlow totally wanted to marry Fanny, but she flat-out turned him down with the eighteenth-century version of the It's Not You, It's Me speech—which is basically the same as the twenty-first-century version, only during the "It's not you" part, you reassure the person that you have no doubts of their worthiness, and in the "It's me" section, you give them leave to think you singular, odd, queer, nay, even whimsical.

No one in Fanny's immediate circle of family and friends was happy about this oddly stubborn, pigheaded decision of hers. Her older sister, Hetty, was particularly pissed. He seemed nice and sensible, this Thomas Barlow. Why the negativity? Her suspiciously young-looking musician father refused to play the will-they-won't-they game for a while, which makes sense because the guy was a busy man. He had eight children to support, a cranky, passive-aggressive second wife, music lessons to give, books to write, and in his spare time he liked to hang out with socialites and famous people no one today has really heard of, like Samuel Johnson, Joshua Reynolds, and David Garrick. But eventually, on behalf of the patriarchy, he jumped in and picked a side. He desired Fanny not to be "*peremptory*" in rejecting the poor guy; and after that, misery ensued. So much misery that one of Fanny's biographers, who shall remain nameless because in my opinion she's kind of a judgmental bitch, accuses Fanny of being—again, at this critical juncture in her life—"a trifle hysterical." Then she goes on to totally diss her for being weak.

But if you ask me, she was actually being quite strong.

Faced with the very real prospect of having to marry some strange, inarticulate guy she barely knew, Frances Burney, Mother of English Fiction, did indeed become a bit hysterical. She lost it. She wigged out. That is a matter of historical fact. It's not open for debate. But once the crisis was over, she did not hesitate. She did not falter.

She chose to stay home, be a spinster, and write something.

Something called *Evelina*, which people still read 225 years later.

Not a lot of people.

Not tons.

Just a few mentally unbalanced TV writers and assorted English majors at East Coast liberal arts colleges.

Which isn't bad when you think about it.

You know, in literary-immortality terms.

And when she was two-thirds done with her bid for literary immortality, the young Miss Frances Burney, spinster, of the parish of St. Martin in the Fields, enlisted the help of her younger brother, Charles—aka Carlos, who would eventually become one of many black sheep in the Burney family, but at this point in our story was basically just a college freshman who drank too much and liked to gamble—and he delivered the manuscript of said novel-in-progress to Thomas Lowndes, bookseller, of Fleet Street, and a couple days later Lowndes wrote back, thinking the author of this anonymous work was a guy, and said...

Sir
I've read & like the Manuscript & if you'll
send the rest I'll soon run it over.

Which reads almost exactly as if it had been sent by my agent on his Blackberry, except that, you know, it's very positive and encouraging, and it seems to imply that someone has actually written something and that someone else is going to disseminate that work to the general public in an incredibly expeditious fashion, thereby skipping the traditional Hollywood step of no one ever getting back to you about your screenplay and you just sitting around waiting and wondering for months on end. And that, my friend, is the one hundred percent true story of how Frances Burney invented the chick-lit genre and actually *became*, as Virginia Woolf once called her, the Mother of English Fiction. Even though I'm sure we all wished she'd invented some cooler, hipper, more impressive-sounding genre, like, I don't know, the buddy action comedy.

MONDAY, JULY 17, 2006

OKAY, SO NOW nearly a month has gone by and tons
of shit has happened, and I haven't written any of it
down, and that *could* be a sign that I'm really busy and
my mental health is improving. Or, guess what else it
could be?

What will you find if you start Googling the phrase
"olfactory groove meningioma"?

A short list of symptoms.

Check this out...

Loss of smell (anosmia)
Subtle personality changes
Mild difficulty with memory
Euphoria
Diminished concentration

Did you catch that last one? Diminished concentration. I think I might have that. I'm reasonably certain I
don't have the euphoria. I'm still waiting—hopefully, as
in filled with hope—for the subtle personality changes,
but I'm starting to think I might have the diminished
concentration.

Although it's not like I've just been sitting around
doing nothing this whole time.

I have been rather busy.

A couple weeks ago, I got my first story assignment,

and last week I wrote an outline. This makes me sound like a conscientious, efficient sixth grader, but I swear that's how we actually do things in the world of professional television writing. The story I got wasn't one I particularly liked, but whatever. I made the best of it. Very often in professional TV writing, you get assigned a story you don't particularly care for, but it's your job to write it, so you soldier on and try to make the best of it and make it your own. Sometimes, by the end of this process, once the script is finished and shot and it airs on national television, or sometimes even *years* later when you walk to your mailbox and find a foreign-residual check, you eventually discover that you don't *mind* the story so much. But in this case, the story in question has a lot of fart jokes in it—more than I generally like to have recourse to, as an artist—so I doubt that in my heart of hearts I will ever reach a point when I truly love this story.

Nonetheless, I soldiered on.

I turned in the outline last Friday, and this morning, this Monday morning, mind you, my boss spent a good fifteen minutes standing in the doorway of my office having the obligatory How Was Your Weekend chat and discussing the cocktail party we're all *required* to go to tonight at the Ritz-Carlton in Pasadena, and never once did he mention this outline.

It was kinda like the whole thing never happened.

Like he never assigned the outline.

Like I never turned it in.

Like we were just a couple of TV-writer acquaintances having a chat at the car wash while waiting for our foreign cars to be detailed.

And, sure, I suppose *I* could have broached the topic. The opening was certainly there, what with all the obligatory talk about our weekends, but it seemed, etiquette-wise, like the ball was in his court.

Him being the boss and all.

So I said nothing, and he said nothing, and then after a while too much time had passed to even think about bringing it up. At that point, the outline basically became like this one-night stand neither one of us wanted to acknowledge. And, being a spinster and all, I'm not supergood at one-night stands, so I changed the subject to how I might possibly be a little late getting back from lunch Wednesday without explicitly explaining why—you know, because I have to drive to Beverly Hills and have another MRI of my head.

Can you believe it's been six months already?

I know I can't. Six months since I made the mature, responsible, and thoroughly informed medical decision to *ignore* my brain tumor and focus all my time and energy on writing a romantic comedy screenplay. You remember my screenplay, right? The one I wrote back in the spring with so much assistance from that how-to-write-a-screenplay book, *Rules for Romantic Comedy*? Well, this probably won't come as a huge shock to you, but it looks like everybody who is anybody has now passed on my screenplay.

Yes, it's official. The two biggest Jennifers represented by my agency aren't interested. So I guess that dream is over. No chariot awaits to swoop me out of TV and into the more prestigious realm of features. I guess I'm sad about it—I can't really tell. I mean, I did put a shitload of time and energy into that thing. The story was inspired by something kinda-sorta real that actually did happen to my friend Kitten after her mom died, and even though I broke Rule #14 and kept the True Love Interest *off-screen* until page twenty-five, I thought it had a lot of potential. In retrospect—now that a certain Meryl Streep movie has come out and made a bazillion dollars at the box office—I can see that it probably wasn't the smartest idea to dress my heroine up in baggy sweaters and have her carry a tote bag. Duh, right? What was I thinking? Once again, I seem to have underestimated how much people seem to give a shit about really expensive shoes.

But whatever. Moving on. That's all you can do, right? As penance for this mistake, I broke down a couple weeks ago—like a prisoner with Stockholm syndrome—and bought myself a new pair of $210 shoes to wear to the insane cocktail party that I am *required* to go to tonight at the Ritz-Carlton in Pasadena. My only consolation is that my new friend Jill will also be attending.

Jill is the other female TV writer on the show who does not wear $500 shoes or sleep with actors, and somehow, over the course of the past month, she and I seem to have become friends. In romantic comedy terms, this is not as good as having an actual Love Interest enter the picture, but a workplace best friend is clearly a major step forward (e.g., Stanley Tucci in *The Devil Wears Expensive Shoes*).

Jill's slightly older than I am, which makes her almost ten years older than the shoe girls, and instead of being a pithy gay man, she's a married-with-kids straight lady from the Valley. When we first met, she asked me if I was married—which totally threw me for a loop. I always assume my spinster thing shows, but maybe it's only detectable to other spinsters. I'm not quite sure how I managed to secure Jill as a valuable addition to the cast of my personal, private rom-com, except that at the end of my first day in the writers' room (after she'd already been working with the shoe girls for an entire week, and I was still really jet-lagged because I had just gotten back from China), she walked right up to me and she said...

JILL

Thank god you're here! Now they can make fun of you for being square.

That was our Meet Cute, and since then we've been

going to lunch together every day at the commissary just outside the lot, the one with the better salad bar, where we chatter away for an hour about books or people we both know or other jobs we've had before that were better than this one.

Jill seems to have had a lot of those.

Me, not so many.

No, all of my previous jobs in TV have been pretty much exactly like this one: strange cliques in the writers' room, bosses who don't acknowledge the existence of your outline, actors who don't want to say their lines, etc., etc., &c. Back when I was just starting out, back in my long-lost early thirties, I tended to get super upset about stuff like that—but, god, that's exhausting. And time-consuming. Who's got time for that, plus a brain tumor *and* a fibroid near my left ovary—which, by the way, is exactly what that gynecological thing turned out to be. Unlike the brain surgeon, my gynecologist didn't really give me any "options" for dealing with it. She basically told me to come back in six months and have another ultrasound. More watch and wait. More driving to Beverly Hills. Which I have to do *again* next Wednesday for the brain tumor; only now I've gotta do it from Burbank, on my lunch hour. So, that led me to tell Jill the full and complete truth about the brain tumor.

And I also kinda told Dave, the writers' assistant.

But that was mostly just an accident.

You see, Dave is very quiet. After six or seven weeks now of knowing him, I think I can safely say that's his main defining characteristic, and so as Jill and I were finishing up our brain tumor walk 'n' talk, I didn't realize at first that he was sitting right there in the writers' room, dutifully waiting for us all to come back from lunch. So I just kept talking about the brain tumor—how it was discovered, how I have to have another MRI on Wednesday, what a pain in the ass it is to drive to Beverly Hills, should I take Coldwater coming back, etc., etc., &c. You know, *as if Dave weren't there*. Which is an incredibly rude thing to do, and it's even ruder when the person you're doing it to is an assistant, which I used to be and so was Jill, and so that makes one more thing we've bonded over: being nice to the assistants, relatively inexpensive footwear, and a conviction that it's just *nicer* if the showrunner acknowledges the existence of the outline you turned in. He doesn't have to love it or anything. He just has to acknowledge that it exists. Like I always try to do with other human beings, except in this one instance when I was kinda rude to Dave, the writers' assistant, who is the last person in the world I would ever want to offend because of my personal credo about always being nice to the assistants and because—well, I can't quite explain this, but I feel sort of strangely drawn to Dave. He is not as young as I first thought when I met him back in June, and he seems to have read a lot of books written before 1900,

and it makes me cringe whenever our boss turns to him
every five seconds in the room and says...

SHOWRUNNER
(panicked, urgent)
Did you get that, Dave?

Because I know, having talked to him a couple
times after work, that he is incredibly well-read, extremely intelligent, and amazingly overqualified for the
job he currently holds, so I just *assume* that he's gotten
everything down. After all, it's his job to sit there all
day and type up everything we say, and most of the
stuff we say:

a) isn't that brilliant
b) gets repeated a zillion times, and
c) could easily be reconstructed on the off-chance
   that he did not get it down because he was
   instant-messaging with the PAs about the
   coffee order or buying concert tickets online.

So, that's odd, right? This inexplicable pull I feel
toward Dave, the writers' assistant. Or maybe it is not
so inexplicable. Maybe it's totally and completely one
hundred percent *explicable*. Because even though it's not
really fair to generalize about people based on how they
look and act and talk and dress and where they went
to college and what sort of concerts they buy tickets
to—well, if we're going to play that game, then I guess
I would have to say that Dave, the writers' assistant,

looks and acts and talks and dresses just *exactly* like the sort of person who might have gone to college with me at the less-famous Ivy League school I attended. Most likely, he would have lived in one of the cool dorms that didn't have air conditioning, and during college he would have dated one of my friends, and then after college he would have come with her to one of the parties my roommate and I used to have back in Brooklyn, and guess what?

He is that sort of person.

In fact, he's *exactly* that sort of person, and I'm not just imagining that and projecting all this stuff onto him because I am:

a) crazy

b) brain-tumor-ridden, and

c) filled with nostalgia for the days before I moved to LA and got ahead in the entertainment industry.

No, I know this for a fact because one of the times we were chatting after work, he said, and I quote...

DAVE
My girlfriend knows someone who
knows you.

And this turned out to be one hundred percent true.

His girlfriend knows my friend Leila, who knows my friend Ed, who used to date my roommate when I lived in Brooklyn. And even though I didn't actually know Leila back when I lived in Brooklyn, Leila also happens to be really good friends with Ed's old roommate, Harry. And you know how Harry and Leila actually know each other? You know what socioeconomic force brought them together?

They used to work at an alternative newspaper.

So it's a small world is the point of that story.

And it's an even smaller world if at any point during the 1990s you lived in Brooklyn or worked at an alternative newspaper or—god forbid—did both. Like I did back in my misspent youth. And that's why I am not making any of this up about Dave. He really is just exactly the sort of person I used to know in my old life, my past life—my life *before* I moved to LA and became such a moderate success in the entertainment industry. And that means I was right about him. One hundred percent completely and utterly right. So when he told me that thing about his girlfriend, I should have *felt* right...right? I should have felt vindicated—you know, for stereotyping him so accurately based entirely on how he dresses and what bands he listens to—but instead I felt this really strange, non-spinster-like feeling it took me forever to identify: I felt disappointed that he had a girlfriend. Huh. Go figure.

Tuesday, August 1, 2006

Shit.

Slight setback at work.

I kinda lost it last Thursday, right before I left for my high school reunion, and I became a bit mentally unhinged, and I—double shit.

My high school reunion.

I totally forgot to set that up, didn't I? Damn. That had some real rom-com second-act-set-piece potential. You know, if only I had been a little more proactive and hired someone to impersonate my fiancé. Thank god nothing major happened that required setting up. Like I didn't meet the man of my dreams or anything. My mom suggested something to that effect as I was leaving the house Saturday night. She said something vaguely hopeful about how I looked nice and maybe I might "meet someone." But instead what happened was that I walked into the banquet hall next to the bowling alley wearing a sleeveless, faux-wrap dress I never would have had the courage to wear in LA, and within seconds of my arrival—seconds, I tell you—the best-looking guy in the room came right up to me and told me he loved my shoes.

Because, as I may have mentioned before, I have a pretty good rapport with the gays.

And mind you, these were not $500 shoes. Or even $200 shoes. No, these were just some $49 shoes I got at that discount shoe warehouse place up on Sunset. You know, the one by the In-N-Out Burger.

So that's kinda the high school reunion in a nutshell. I'm glad I went. There were tons of people there I hadn't seen in a long time. Most of the women seemed like they had already met the man of their dreams. And now they were divorced and trying to work out some sort of shared-custody agreement.

And the guys?

Well, mostly I talked to the married guys, although I assure you I wasn't seeking them out. No, they basically just kept coming up to me all night and asking if I remembered them and apologizing profusely for the fact that their *wives* really wanted to meet me. And then a wife would appear—generally this was someone I did *not* go to high school with—and she would turn out to be a huge fan of the show I'm currently working on, which was great for my ego because it would be a real drag to spend twenty years living in big cities, listening to public radio, and reinventing yourself as a New York/Jewish intellectual only to return to the basketball-loving Midwestern town you grew up in and have lots of conversations that start, "Well, it's on cable..." or "It's with this guy who used to be on *Veronica's Closet*."

Plus, you know, I weigh a lot less now than I did in high school and just generally look about ten thousand times better. So even though I don't wear makeup or expensive shoes or straighten my hair or wax my nether regions like a porn star, for thirty-six hours last weekend I actually got to feel kinda hot.

You know, by northwest Indiana standards.

That happens sometimes when I travel. Sometimes—in other cities—I get the feeling that maybe I am not so very hideous to look at.

But the feeling always passes when I return to LA.

Not that I'm complaining or anything. I swore I wasn't going to do that anymore. You know, complain about contemporary, twenty-first-century LA. Truly, it is not very gracious of me. Especially when you consider that I don't *have* to live here. I mean, sure, I have to live here if I want to continue being a moderately successful TV writer, but I could always be like Mickey Sachs in *Hannah and Her Sisters* and give up my fancy, well-paying TV-writing job. That plot move is totally available to me now that I actually *have* a fancy, well-paying TV-writing job. It probably wouldn't have worked out so well earlier in the year—you know, back when I was unemployed. But now that I actually have the sort of job millions of people would die for, I could easily quit it and go on some sort of religious odyssey and possibly discover the meaning of life at a Marx Brothers movie and maybe even fall in love with someone.

Or I could just pack up and move back to the Rust Belt, where the general population is not so inordinately obsessed with body-fat ratios and personal grooming.

I heard a story like that once. A contemporary,

twenty-first-century LA fairy tale about a single, successful TV writer-girl who gave up her fancy, well-paying job, moved to Chicago, and married a very nice fat guy. I'm not sure I believe it. It sounds apocryphal to me. Like it might be a parable made up by some very nice fat guy in order to discourage women from trying to get ahead in Hollywood. Even if it's true, that particular story line would never work for me, personally, because guess what? I have already lived in Chicago. For three whole years. And the entire time I was there, much to my mother's dismay, no guys—fat or thin—ever evinced any desire to marry me.

So for the moment, I'm sticking with LA. It suits me. It allows me to feel *right* all the time about how empty and god-awful and image-obsessed the world is, and that's a huge accomplishment for a metropolis—a huge boon to the mental health of its spinster population. Plus, we have tons of great brain surgeons here, and that has become a lot more important to me now that my brain tumor is getting bigger.

Not a lot bigger.

Not tons.

But, you know, bigger than it was in January.

I discovered this fun fact last Thursday, when I drove to Beverly Hills and had my second meeting with the first brain surgeon. He started by putting the MRI up on the little screen—you know, just like they do on TV. And then he told me that the tumor was getting bigger and tried to show me exactly where it was, which is another thing they always do on TV, but of course I couldn't really tell what the hell he was talking about. It all just looked like a lot of marshmallow fluff, so I nodded and smiled and waited patiently for the brain surgeon to tell me what the fuck I should do about my brain tumor.

Because that's another thing that tends to happen all the time on TV.

But once again he did not do that.

He didn't even come close.

He basically just said the exact same thing he said last time. You know, about how it was all *my* choice, about how I had to be the one to decide. Only this time when he said it, I swear there was this little glint in his eye. This little spark of amusement. Like he's so incredibly smart—he is, after all, a brain surgeon—that he figured out on my first visit how desperately I want him to be in charge and have an opinion and tell me what to do. So now on this, our second, visit, he's even more perversely determined *not* to be in charge and *not* to have an opinion and *not* to tell me what to do.

And I gotta say, I really dig that about him.

More and more, after this second visit, I am feeling secure in my assessment that this particular brain surgeon is The One. After all, he did say—given that my tumor seems to be growing very slowly and I am (at least to a brain surgeon) relatively young—that he didn't think it would be a problem to wait another year to have it removed. And then when I asked him if there were any really compelling reasons why I *shouldn't* wait another year to have it removed, he replied, without hesitating...

```
            BRAIN SURGEON
      Sure. I could wake up tomorrow
      and get hit by a bus.
                  (beat)
      And then you'd have to find
      yourself another brain surgeon.
```

And I dug that, too. Because really *good* brain surgeons should also have a dark, twisted sense of humor, don't you think? At least they always seem to on TV.

The only trouble is, now I'm right back where I started.

I still can't get anyone in a position of authority to tell me what to do about my brain tumor, and I must have been kinda upset about this when I showed up late to work last Thursday morning, because I ran into one of the shoe girls when I was parking my car in my designated space, and she looked concerned and asked me if something was wrong. So I said yes and somehow the whole story about the brain tumor just came pouring out of me. We even went into her office and closed the door, which is generally a sign on a TV show that a bunch of people are getting together to talk about how badly the TV show is being run by the current showrunner. But in this case it was actually more about the brain tumor, although at one point she did suggest *telling* the current showrunner about the brain tumor.

So I did.

I don't know how to explain it except that this particular shoe girl has a real take-charge way about her. If she tells you to do something, you do it—*even if you don't want to do it*—and that probably explains why she's way more successful than I am at our chosen profession. She takes charge of things and tells people what to do—indeed, she seems to sorta kinda *enjoy* telling people what to do. And I gotta say I respect her for that. I do.

Almost as much as I respect her for dropping out of the shoe contest.

You see, it's been superhot here lately—like it usually is in Burbank in August—and finally, she just couldn't take walking huge distances across the lot in heels anymore, and so for two days in a row she wore the exact same pair of really cute glen plaid Chuck Taylor slip-ons—you know, the ones with elastic instead of the laces—and just like that, she was out.

Out of the shoe contest!

Although, she has sold two pilots to major television networks this development season, so all in all, I think she's probably feeling okay about being out of the shoe contest. After all, the winner of the ridiculous contest known as "development season" gets to have her pilot made and maybe even wins the ultimate grand prize of getting to have her own TV show on the air; the winner of the shoe contest just gets a new pair of shoes from Barneys.

So now it's over.

Not the shoe contest.

The shoe contest is still going on.

But my big secret about the brain tumor is officially over. After I told the showrunner about it, I went into the writers' room and told everybody else. They all seem to be taking it okay. Although I'm sure on some level the showrunner has got to be thinking...

           SHOWRUNNER (V.O.)
     I can't believe I hired the girl
     with the brain tumor!

But of course now it's too late to fire me. You can't fire the girl with the brain tumor. And you also can't fire the girl with the pay-or-play clause in her contract. Can you believe that? Can you believe that I, who am only a moderately successful television writer, actually have a pay-or-play clause in my contract? I just found that out the other day from Arnie Greenblatt. I should probably listen more when he talks. Also, I should probably read the contracts before I sign them. I swear I had no idea about this. A pay-or-play clause means they have to pay you *even if they fire you*, and I've always assumed that only the really *successful* TV writers have clauses like that in their contracts, but apparently I have one too. They've made some sort of exception in my case, which works out well from my perspective, because now I can spend even *less* time worrying about getting fired and more time worrying about the brain tumor pressing on my frontal lobe. I totally wish I had known about this last month when I turned in my outline and my boss failed to acknowledge its existence until we found ourselves completely starved for conversation at that terrible cocktail party we were *required* to attend to launch the new network.

Damn. A fancy party! Yet another lost opportunity for a rom-com second-act set piece. Truly, it wasn't much of a thrill. I mean the part when he told me he liked my outline was good, but the rest of it was kind of a drag. The shoe girls had all left early that day and gone over to change their clothes together at one of their houses. I was kinda impressed by that, because it seemed like something girls would do *in a movie*. You know, change their clothes together. I gotta hand it to them, too. Whatever they did to each other en masse like that really worked. They all looked really good. Particularly the really tall, really blond, really skinny one. I know this because I ended up hanging out that night with the only guy I know in LA who has ever kinda-sorta even halfheartedly tried to sleep with me, and his main topic of conversation all night was how good the really tall, really blond, really skinny one looked and variations on that theme, like could I introduce her to him.

Which is probably within his rights.

After all, the guy has been trying halfheartedly to sleep with me for like ten years now, and I've been blowing him off for ten years because he's basically my friend and he's totally nice and all that but—shit, how to put this tactfully?

He sleeps with prostitutes.

And I don't want to judge, but that just doesn't work with my genre of choice.

Think about it.

Suppose a thirtysomething rom-com heroine *were* to drink too much at a work-related cocktail function filled with network executives and television critics, and end up sleeping with some guy who also sleeps with prostitutes. You don't exactly have to be a professional writer to know where that setup is going. Surely she would catch some incurable disease, right? Or quite possibly end up becoming a prostitute herself. And I don't know if you've noticed, but I don't really have time for anymore diseases at the moment. My plate is full. Plus, that setup doesn't say "romantic comedy" to me. That doesn't scream *Hannah and Her Sisters*. That's an indie film that plays for only one week at the Sunset Five, and I'm the only one who goes to see it because it got a good review in the *Weekly*, or maybe it stars some young actor I used to work with and I always try to support her whenever she does something edgy.

No, in my genre of choice—in romantic comedies—leading men don't sleep with prostitutes. They are occasionally allowed to stop and ask prostitutes for directions, but I'm pretty sure that's not how the whole prostitute thing got started with this guy, because the way he always explains it to me, it seems like you call them on the phone and they come directly to your house. You know, *Risky Business*-style. So there's very little chance of anyone getting lost and needing directions, and so if you are thinking...

```
            SELF (V.O.)
   At last! Finally! A love
   interest! Sleep with him! Sleep
   with that guy!
```

...don't. Don't think that. Because it's not happening. I have come way too far with The Spinster Way to just give up on it one random summer night in the backyard of the Ritz-Carlton in Pasadena. And for what? For the thrill of sleeping with some guy who has spent the entire night talking to me in a self-pitying way about how incredibly hot all the other girls at the party are? I, personally, think that when you put those two things in the balance, The Spinster Way comes out way ahead. After all, with The Spinster Way, you get to go home early and leave with your self-respect, and with the other way—well, I've never really tried the other way, so I'm not real clear on what its supposed advantages are. That is the giant, overarching GirlWorld mystery I have yet to solve, although I will admit that in the two months since I started this job that millions want, this job where I have to spend all day, every day, in the general orbit of the shoe girls, I have been picking up a lot of useful new information about how to be and look and talk and act less like myself, less like a spinster, and more like your average, everyday resident of GirlWorld. I'm not sure I will ever want to apply this information, but I'm taking it all down just in case.

THURSDAY, SEPTEMBER 7, 2006

I HAVE JUST been asked to leave the set by one of the actors.

This has never happened to me before, so I'm not exactly sure what I'm supposed to do. I've been *ignored* by actors, had them fail to acknowledge my existence, that type of thing. But being asked to leave the set is a totally new experience for me, so now I'm just sitting here in my office trying to figure out what my next move should be. It's barely 7 a.m., so the place is totally dead. It'll be hours before any of the other writers—or even any of the assistants—show up and join me. Like if Dave were here, I could go stand by his desk and talk to him about the Richard Hawley CD he loaned me or something that was on TV last night, but since he's not here—since no one is here—and the episode they are filming today is one hundred percent completely and totally my responsibility, I should probably be mature about this whole thing and march right back across the lot to the very set I was just kicked off of.

Or I could just wait here in my office a little while longer and keep Journaling for Anxiety™.

~

I'm still not exactly sure how this happened. The day started off so promising. I parked in my designated parking space. I found the right stage. I found a place on the sidelines where I could watch the rehearsal, yet not be too close. That's my *philosophy* of how to be a writer on the set of a TV show. I like to be present, but largely unseen. I'm sure other TV writers have their own philosophies, but that's mine. I got it from Flaubert, who never really spent much time on the set, although in a letter to his mistress he once wrote, "The author in his book must be like God in his universe, everywhere present and nowhere visible."

So there I was, trying as hard as possible to be invisible, when the first AD asked everyone to leave the set so that the first rehearsal could be a *private* rehearsal, with just the actors and the director. That seemed rather strange to me because by the time you get past year three of a long-running American TV series, everybody involved in the proceedings is generally so completely and totally over the whole fucking thing that the only time you would ever really need to have a "private" rehearsal is if you were doing some sort of sex scene.

And this was not any sort of sex scene.

I know because I wrote it—or at least I wrote the first draft of it, before it got rewritten by the showrunner and possibly one or two of the shoe girls. I'm not totally clear on how the rewrite process works around here, but whatever. Some shows you get to be involved in your own rewrites. Some shows you don't. I've worked both ways, and while there is a certain amount of artistic satisfaction that can be derived from having actually written the thing that says "Written by You" in the opening credits, in a way I think it's better—*if you happen to have any sort of tumor*—to be working on the second type of show. That way you don't have to be too involved with the proceedings past the first round of notes. Sure, there are meetings to go to: production meetings, tone meetings, casting sessions. But the main thing you, the professional TV writer, have to do at these meetings is pretend you actually wrote the script and answer questions about it, and nowadays I'm an old hand at that kind of stuff. I can do it in my sleep. That's what makes this particular job such a good one for a girl with a brain tumor. Because at this job, once you turn in your second draft, you can—in good conscience—wash your hands of the whole thing and start concentrating full-time on your list of questions to ask the brain surgeon.

~

The brain surgeon predicted this might happen.

Not that I would get kicked off the set. No one could have predicted that. I swear I was just standing there doing nothing wrong. No, he said that people tend to realize in the car, when they are driving home from the brain surgeon, that there were a zillion questions they totally meant to ask, and so he told me I could call him if I thought of any. Originally, I *was* going to do that. I was just going to call. But when I tried that, Cynthia, the very nice lady who answered the phone, said that it would be better if I *faxed* the questions. So that set me back a few weeks, because I don't know if this is true of the general population of brain tumor sufferers, but if you are a professional writer who is used to being graded and judged and criticized and "noted" and sometimes even openly mocked for the things you put down on paper—well, sometimes it can be very hard to put things down on paper.

Except when you're Journaling for Anxiety™.

Then naturally you can just write whatever the fuck you want in a totally stream-of-consciousness style with no rules you have to follow and zero percent chance of getting fired.

Of course, now that I think about it, that's also true in my current job. I actually *can't* be fired right now. I mean I can, but since I have that pay-or-play clause in my contract, it's pretty unlikely. It's not like my first script went over *that* badly. I got rewritten, sure, but some of it is still me—some romantic banter on a rooftop, a few lines here and there—so I should probably seize this moment to do a quick TV-writer victory lap. Apparently, there's this condition called Imposter Syndrome, where you walk around all the time feeling like you are not the successful doctor, lawyer, or co-executive producer that people within your industry widely perceive you to be, and that any second now, you will be exposed as a complete fraud. I think I've got that. You know, in addition to a fibroid on my left ovary and a brain tumor pressing on my frontal lobe. That's why I turned to leave this morning when the first AD asked everyone to clear the set for the "private" rehearsal. Leaving was my first instinct, my gut reaction—but then she stopped me and said...

FIRST ASSISTANT DIRECTOR
Not you. You can stay. You're
the writer.

And an actor who happened to be standing nearby jokingly agreed with her. She was all like...

SUPERSWEET ACTOR-GIRL
Yeah, you're the writer.

So for about ten seconds, I felt kind of cool.
Confident.
Capable.
In charge.
Until another one of the actors crossed the set, walked straight toward me, and for a split second I thought maybe—just maybe—she was going to say "Hello" or "Good morning," but instead she just asked me, point-blank, to leave.
So I did.

In the end, they weren't very good.

My questions for the brain surgeon.

Still, they had to be asked.

They had to be asked because once you break down like a crazy person and start telling everyone in your immediate vicinity about your brain tumor—everybody at work, your old college friends, your married sisters in the Midwest—well, then you start to get a lot of *advice* about your brain tumor. Serious conversations start to happen. Tons of emails fly back and forth. And after about, let's say...I don't know...five weeks' worth of these *serious conversations*, you start to think maybe— just maybe—you should go ahead and have brain surgery and get the fucking thing removed because either:

a) it would go fine, and then you could put all this behind you, or

b) you would die, and then you could put all this behind you, or

c) you would end up a vegetable attached to a bunch of machines somewhere in the Midwest.

But in all these scenarios, the serious conversations would stop.

And what a relief that would be.

They all start out exactly the same. The first thing

everybody wants to know is how I found out about the brain tumor. That's usually when I try to explain to them about *Hannah and Her Sisters*, the big band music, the series of tests leading to a brain scan, etc., etc., &c. But a surprisingly large number of people can't remember the plot of *Hannah and Her Sisters*. Often, they confuse it with *Crimes and Misdemeanors*, which is also good but doesn't have any TV writers or brain tumors in it, just a rabbi with a degenerative eye disease. Of course, in *Hannah*, Mickey's "tumor" isn't actually a tumor; it's just a spot on his X-ray that freaks him out and causes him to reexamine his life and think about becoming a Catholic. I, sadly, am already Catholic. Not practicing or anything, but it's safe to say that I am currently in possession of way more confirmation names than a neurotic-writer type generally has in a Woody Allen movie. Plus, my tumor actually *is* a tumor, and in retrospect it is kinda surprising that I found out about it, because I'm not a well-known hypochondriac who goes running to doctors at the drop of a hat. The only reason I broke down and called my ridiculously suave ENT last December was that my ears got all clogged up—like when you're on an airplane—and they wouldn't unclog even though I took an antihistamine, and then I began to be plagued by these weird vertigo incidents. Plus, that same week, while I was co–executive-producing the last episode of an already canceled TV show, getting tons of network notes on my pilot, and trying to figure out how the fuck I would possibly rewrite it for the nineteenth time, I threw up in the private bathroom attached to my gigantic office on the Sunset/Gower lot. That's when I finally cracked and called the ENT. But he's in complete agreement with Brain Surgeon #1 that a tiny little benign brain tumor pressing on my olfactory nerve wouldn't actually *cause* any of those weird things to happen. Nope. Apparently, throwing up in your fancy office and vertigo are both signs of stress. That was a new one on me. Throwing up, sure. People are *constantly* throwing up in Hollywood, not just the actresses with eating disorders. But vertigo?

Anyway, that's question number one about the brain tumor: origin story. After that, people always go straight to cell phones and Diet Coke. Seriously, Diet Coke comes up *all the time*, and if I were the people who make Diet Coke, I might want to look into that. Me, I've always preferred coffee. Or, if not always, at least since the early nineties, when I moved from New York to Chicago and developed an obsessive crush on a goateed latte guy who worked at the Starbucks on Diversey. Before that, I did drink my fair share of Diet Coke, but it's never been my drug of choice, so I highly doubt it caused the brain tumor. In truth, I will probably never know what caused the brain tumor.

Although I suspect it may have been season three of the teenage melodrama.

Kidding. Totally kidding.

Season three of the teenage melodrama really wasn't that bad. For instance, no one ever asked me to leave the set. That never happened. Although, once someone asked me how much money I made. Very pointedly. In front of like a zillion people. And that was worse, in a lot of ways, than being asked to leave the set, because at least when you are asked to leave the set, *you get to leave the set*. And what a glorious treat that is. I mean, I know it sounds glamorous and all, but in my experience, the set is basically just a place where people walk right up to you and criticize your work in an incredibly blunt, inelegant manner, and sometimes they even ask you to *redo* your work right there, on the spot, while the entire crew is standing around staring at you and waiting to shoot something. Plus, there is often an outdoorsy, camping-type element to the proceedings. Like maybe you're in a field somewhere and there's a creek nearby and the weather's probably shitty, so you better be wearing sensible shoes, wool socks, etc. Basically, the whole thing is just not very me, which is why I'm still sitting here Journaling for Anxiety™ even though it's after 8 now. The crew is probably done lighting, and I'm sure the actors have been through hair and makeup, and pretty soon they will start shooting the scene that has been privately rehearsed. Presumably the actor who asked me to leave feels good about having made her point—whatever that was—and it's not like she expects me to not return to the set ever again over the course of my episode.

Or maybe she does.

Now that I think about it, that very same actor also came to see my boss last Friday and let it be known in no uncertain terms that she really hates my script.

But for a wide variety of reasons, I didn't take that too personally.

You see, it's really not all that uncommon for an actor on a long-running American TV show to "hate" a script, and if you're lucky enough to be a writer on a long-running American TV show, it's inevitable that one of yours is going to get hated. You would think—because of that law of physics with the equal and opposite reactions, and all that—that the reverse would be true as well. You know, that every once in a while one of your scripts would get loved. But that almost never happens. Being hated is the far more common reaction, and all you can really do when it's your turn to be hated is suck it up and take it, and that's pretty easy to do because—well, because they pay you a lot to be hated. Also, if you do a little digging, you will generally discover that the reason the actor in question really hates your script is less about you—your talents as a writer, the nuances of your storytelling, the rhythms of your dialogue—and more about There Is a Dog in the Scene or Why Is the Call Time So Early? or I Don't Want to Work with That Other Actor or There Is a Party I

Would Like to Go to That Night So Could We Cut That Scene Entirely? Stuff like that. On the teenage melodrama, I used to file all these complaints under a category called Petty Bitchery, and if you are a person who is not descended from a long line of rich people and you have to, you know, *work for a living*, then you've probably had some doings with Petty Bitchery. It's very big in offices. Super popular in workplaces all across the country. And so I'm sure *that* explains why that actor asked me to leave the set this morning.

It didn't really have anything to do with me.

She was just having a bad day, or maybe she wants to leave early today or wait...shit. I think I just figured something out. What if this was one of those "test" situations where someone behaves kind of shitty to you and the thing you're *supposed* to do is behave shitty right back to them, and then they respect you? Fuck. This has happened to me before on other shows, and it's always had to be explained to me after the fact that I have botched the situation by not behaving shitty back to the other person. You'd think that I would learn from these mistakes, but somehow I never do.

Shit.

Shit.

Shit.

I should probably go.

Long List of Questions to Ask the Brain Surgeon

How many times have you performed this exact surgery?

Is the tumor hard to reach or in any way complicated to remove?

Does the surgery become more complicated the longer I wait to have it?

Could the tumor be affecting my spelling? Like the other day for a second I couldn't remember how to spell "knot." And right now I'm not too sure about "affecting." Should it be "effecting"? In general, I've found it harder over the past couple years to remember how to spell words that sound exactly the same but are spelled differently. Homophones, I believe they're called. Like they're/there/their, etc.

Or—and I think this is the more likely scenario—is the above paragraph just

an example of an already anxious
person who is obsessed with words
becoming more and more anxious because
now she knows she has a brain tumor
growing inside her head?

Is the abovementioned anxiety a good
reason to have the surgery sooner
rather than later?

At which hospital would you perform
the surgery?

What is the recovery like?

How long would I need someone to
come stay with me? I live alone,
and I would have to ask one of my
sisters to come from the Midwest—
they are non-pros who have many kids,
responsibilities, etc.

MONDAY, OCTOBER 16, 2006

THE HOLIDAYS ARE a bad time to have brain surgery, right?

I've seen what TV writers are like at that time of year. Also what actors, network executives, agents, and entertainment lawyers are like—and I can only imagine that brain surgeons are roughly the same.

They are all distracted and thinking about their ski vacations.

So...no. Not happening. I have a well-documented, middle-sister tendency to be weak and indecisive and constantly iffing and butting about things, but on this point I'm holding firm...

I'm not having brain surgery during the holidays.

I just can't do it. It can't be done. Both my sisters happen to have vacation that time of year, so it makes sense on a purely practical level. The older one is a teacher, and the younger one is a nurse, and so they both, you know, do good things for society for which they receive very little money. Bizarre, huh? We don't get much of that here in Hollywood. Also, they are both moms, and moms have this tendency to want to schedule shit way in advance. Vacations, major surgeries...they like to pin things down, get them on the books. Spinsters, on the other hand, prefer to go with the flow. Maybe wait till April.

And the brain surgeon totally agreed with me on

this.

When he called me back to answer all those crazy questions I had faxed him, he did concede that anxiety about having brain surgery might be a good reason to have brain surgery sooner rather than later. Score! But he also thought having brain surgery could easily wait until the end of the current TV season. That was his professional opinion as both a brain surgeon and as someone who was once a brain-surgery consultant on a TV show. Clearly Brain Surgeon #1 gets me. That seems obvious, right? I'm not sure that's essential to the brain-surgery process, but I don't think it can possibly hurt, so for a while there I started making these brave, confident pronouncements about how I was going to have brain surgery in April, and that seemed to solve a lot of my second-act problems and move my story forward in an interesting way.

It's not a *huge* plot move, but it definitely counts as a Temporary Triumph (Rule #13) because it put a stop to all the incredibly boring, repetitive scenes I kept having with various supporting players who were pestering me nonstop about having brain surgery.

My married sisters in the Midwest.

My college friends.

My new workplace best friend Jill.

Even a couple of the shoe girls.

Emails.

Phone calls.

Random encounters in the kitchen while I'm trying to figure out how to work the new Keurig machine.

Basically, by telling everyone about my brain tumor, I inadvertently created this huge cast of female supporting characters who feel like it's their raison d'être to pester me all the time about having brain surgery. Like my older, Hannah-like sister keeps pointing out how January is a supergood time for her; and my little sister sent me this long email about how she was trying to get pregnant, and if it worked, by the time April rolled around she would be way too pregnant to come stay with me while I had brain surgery. Then, being the youngest sister, she closed with a suggestion that maybe I, the middle sister, didn't really *want* her to come stay with me while I had brain surgery.

Maybe I really wanted my older, more Hannah-like sister to come stay with me.

Which is totally the kind of shit that happens when a story has three sisters.

In Chekhov.

In Woody Allen.

And definitely in real life.

So that's when I suggested February as a compromise position—what were middle sisters born to do except compromise?—and I guess I can live with February.

I *preferred* April.

But whatever.

It's October now.

Or, as they would call it in *Hannah and Her Sisters*, with white letters on a black title card…"Autumn Chill."

Autumn Chill

Fall isn't exactly great here in LA. It's not like there are wharfs you can sit on where the wind gently blows your hair, and it never gets cold enough to wear a super cute navy blue duffle coat, but if you are on a show that's not completely imploding—low ratings, cast mutinies, entire scripts thrown out by the network at the very last minute—October can actually be a pretty okay time of year.

In TV terms, it's when the last of the pilots get pitched and the first of the showrunners get fired. In fashion terms, it becomes possible, if your calves are thin enough, to wear boots with a skirt. There's a lot to live for in LA in October—particularly, if you are not a showrunner who has just gotten fired or a person who has sold a pilot to a major television network. I feel for those people, I do. Especially the ones who sold a pilot this past development season, because now they all have to start *working* on the pilots they sold this past development season. They have to do all the super annoying pilot-related shit I was doing last year at this time—writing outlines, rewriting outlines, getting notes, etc., etc., &c.—whereas the lazy, unmotivated, brain-tumor-ridden people who didn't even try to sell a pilot this year, those people get to actively *enjoy* October in LA. And if they're not on a show that's imploding—or maybe they are but no one's specifically asked them to do anything about the fact that it's imploding, and it's not really their job to intrude on lots of top-secret meetings that may be happening behind closed doors—well, then they can just spend a lot of sunny October days sitting on the front porch watching the studio tour go by, chatting with the twentysomething assistants about their love lives and occasionally, when there's time, working on their ill-fated, six-part miniseries about Frances Burney, Mother of English Fiction.

It's been a long time since we checked in with Fanny, hasn't it? Don't despair. This is why the Previously On was invented. That's one of my jobs around here. In fact, right now it's kind of my only job. I never got another script assignment, and the story room has stopped convening every day from 10 to 7, so basically my only job right now is to help the assistant editors make the Previously On. For each episode, I start them out with a list of key story points and clips that might work. Then when they have a first pass edited together, I walk over to the post-production trailer and watch it with them and give them notes in what I hope is a kind and encouraging manner. I really like this job. I'm thinking of asking Arnie Greenblatt if there's any way I can turn it into some sort of niche—you know, hire myself out as someone who specializes in the past and just does the Previously On. I've done five of them so far, and they all went over pretty well, so now the Previously On has become like my own personal, private little fiefdom.

I'm sort of like the *showrunner* of the Previously On.

That's right. As we speak, there are approximately thirty to sixty seconds of network television airtime that I am personally responsible for, and to be honest, I think that's about all I can handle. Just those sixty seconds. It's exhausting being responsible for things—TV shows, small children, whatever—and the vim and vigor with which most of the population is running around all the time *pursuing* these sorts of responsibilities is astonishing to me. Like just the other night I had dinner with an old college friend who is doing what most overeducated, non-brain-tumor-ridden women in their late thirties are doing. She's injecting herself with lots of drugs and hormones and embryos and stuff in the hopes of getting pregnant, which must be something she really wants because the process itself doesn't look like very much fun. It seems to make her feel shitty and bloated and forces her to tell lots of really graphic stories about her female parts, and, obviously, you wouldn't put yourself through that kind of thing unless you were super psyched about the outcome.

You know, the part when you have a small child you have to look after for the next twenty years.

Most people seem to be way into that kind of thing. It's very important to them to have things *of their own*, and they're totally willing to go through a lot of annoying shit to get the stuff that is specifically *their own*. Like right now, all the stressed-out, overworked TV writers who are simultaneously working on shows and rebreaking their pilot stories for the sixteenth time— well, those people are doing that because their goal is to have *shows* of their own. They're willing to adopt, if they have to. In a pinch, they'd jump in and run someone else's show and love it and take care of it and try super hard to get it renewed for the next season, but ideally, they would like to have shows *of their own*—just like all these women injecting themselves with stuff want to have babies *of their own*, and presumably all this stuff *of their own* will make them happy, or they wouldn't be going to so much trouble and inconvenience to get it.

I guess my theory about this is that all these people don't understand how nice it is to just sit on the front porch and watch the studio tour go by. Or maybe they don't have an ill-fated, six-part miniseries they are thinking of sending in to the BBC? I just discovered on their website that they accept unsolicited submissions— which no one in contemporary, twenty-first-century LA would ever even think about doing. They probably have to over there because it's a publicly funded company. So what the hell, right? What do I have to lose? It's been at least three months since my rom-com got kicked to the curb. Maybe it's time for me to put myself out there again, risk another rejection? Sure, I'll have to write up an entire proposal, episode summaries, etc., etc., &c. But that can't be that hard, and what's the worst that can happen? Either the BBC will reject my proposal for a lavishly produced, six-part miniseries about Frances Burney, Mother of English Fiction, her creative struggles, her financial woes, and her romantic difficulties, or worse, they will accept it, and then the ill-fated miniseries I have been obsessing on and working out in my head for the past six and a half years will become just another day job that annoys the shit out of me.

So where to begin? How to summarize the fortunes and misfortunes of the famous Miss Burney? How to make them sound glossy and interesting and sell them for a general audience? Actually, this *is* going to be hard. History often faults her for being weak and prissy and anxious—that's the obvious disadvantage of leaving behind all your Journaling for Anxiety™. If you do, you can't pretend, centuries later, to be one of those bold, confident Angelina Jolie–style heroines the industry loves so much: the ones with pouty lips who make action movies. Fanny wasn't like that—she wasn't the sort of "empowered" heroine we seem to like so much here in the twenty-first century. She didn't act all sassy and rude to people. She didn't use her beauty to manipulate men. Because guess what...*Fanny didn't have any beauty*. But all the normal-looking girls who are meek and timid and respectful of the feelings of others? Don't *they* deserve a heroine? Who will represent the anxious? The studious? The shy? Who will tell their stories? That's my goal with my six-part mini series. To give all the normal-looking girls who don't care about shoes someone *they* can look up to.

And, in her own small way, Fanny *was* a revolutionary.

In her early twenties, you may recall, she blew off Thomas Barlow in order to stay home and work on her novel. Or as she put it at the time...

I must again repeat what I have so often had the hardiesse to say, that I have no idea why a single Life may not be happy. Liberty is not without its value—with women as well as with men, though it has not equal recommendations for both,—& I hope never without prospect brighter to myself to lose mine.

Did you catch that? That part about "without prospect brighter to myself"? Basically what she was saying was that her single life at twenty-two was pretty good. She had a day job she really liked as her father's amanuensis—aka secretary or, if we want to be all twenty-first century about it, his assistant. Her hours were not particularly arduous. Her commute was nothing. Her boss was cool. And, unlike a lot of your more lazy, unmotivated twenty-first-century twentysomethings, Fanny didn't seem to mind staying up all night in an ice-cold garret writing and rewriting her chick-lit novel by dim candlelight. So her feeling circa 1775 was that unless some guy came along who totally rocked her world, she didn't particularly care if she ever got married.

If it happened, it happened. If not, eh.

She made an exception in the case of true love, of course. Everyone does. I'm sure I would too if I ever actually encountered some. But if there was any true love in the case of the Thomas Barlow Affair, it was all on Thomas Barlow's side. And after Fanny turned him down, she never looked back, never regretted that decision.

Not when she was twenty-five and still a virgin.

Or even when she was thirty-five and still a virgin.

Indeed, after the Thomas Barlow Affair, Fanny's Journaling for Anxiety™ goes on in excruciating, blog-like detail for six additional decades—sixty-five more years—and never once in all that time does she ever waste a single second angsting or obsessing on Thomas Barlow, dreaming of the other, shadow life she might have led as Mrs. Thomas Barlow, or bullshitting on the front porch with her spinster boss about how Thomas Barlow barely even said hello today when he delivered the copier paper.

So clearly he wasn't the guy for her.

But there were other contenders.

Jeremiah Crutchley makes his first appearance in Part Two of my six-part miniseries, which is where I'm currently stuck—unable to move forward due to medical scanning appointments, career indecision, Journaling for Anxiety™, fear of not having a day job, etc., etc., &c. Plus, my ill-fated attempt to write a traditional, by-the-numbers Hollywood romantic comedy gobbled up three solid months of writing time that might have been more wisely spent writing an eighteenth-century romantic comedy about Fanny Burney and Jeremiah Crutchley. Fanny was twenty-nine the summer she spent hanging out with him at Mrs. Thrale's country house, and twenty-nine is always a dangerous age in GirlWorld. He was thirty-six, loved to hunt, was incredibly lacking in self-confidence, and totally shared Fanny's conviction that Johnson's *Life of Pope* was the best of the Lives— tons better than, say, his *Life of Dryden* or his *Life of*

Swift. He sounds nice, right? And he wasn't *just* nice; he also had this other characteristic that has historically played super well in romantic comedies: *he was rich*. I'm not sure how rich, but he had an estate. You know, like Mr. Darcy in *Pride and Prejudice*. Of course, looks-wise, he was no Colin Firth. We know this because Fanny's BFF Mrs. Thrale once described Jeremiah Crutchley in *her* diaries—which you can also get your hands on if you are *that* obsessed—as "ugly & aukward." Fanny, for her part, never described what Jeremiah Crutchley looked like. But then again, Fanny never described what *anybody* looked like. Not even the characters in her very own novels. This could be a sign of how totally not-shallow she was. How poorly she would have fit in here in contemporary, twenty-first-century LA, because in the end, she cared more about what people were *like*—the content of their characters, their thoughts, their feelings—than about what they looked like.

Or it could just be a sign that she was totally fucking nearsighted.

None of the impoverished academics who study Fanny seem to linger too long on this question, but her diaries are actually *filled* with moments where she's squinting across a crowded room at someone, not exactly sure who they are. You know, as in "*Maybe* that's Edmund Burke?" They definitely had spectacles back then, right? I mean, we've all seen cartoon Ben Franklin wearing his, but I guess it wasn't necessarily considered "proper" to wear them in "company," and lord knows contacts weren't an option, so what was a nearsighted spinster to do back then? In Fanny's case, she usually erred on the side of hanging back and not saying hello to people.

This was probably a smart thing to do, etiquette-wise, because circa 1781, they had tons of super complicated rules about who could talk to whom. But maybe it also explains how she wound up being a spinster in the first place. Makes sense, right? Obviously, if you hang back a lot at parties, you're probably not meeting *tons* of people. You're not, as we would say in the modern parlance, "putting yourself out there." So how *did* the very nearsighted Fanny Burney describe the "ugly & aukward" Jeremiah Crutchley? At the end of May 1781, she said his "first appearance, his coldness, pride, reserve & *sneering* all wear off upon further acquaintance, & leave behind nothing but good humour & good will." By August she was describing him as "one of the worthiest & most amiable creatures in the World, however full of spleen, oddities, and minor foibles," and unlike Thomas Barlow, he doesn't disappear completely from her diaries once his guest star arc is complete. She runs into him again in 1788, when she's a thirty-six-year-old spinster, and here is what she has to say on that occasion...

> *I never knew him, in any essential point, vary from the strictest honour in every notion he ever uttered. He is, indeed, a singular Character; good,*

upright, generous,—yet rough, unpolished, whim-
sical & fastidious: believing all women at his ser-
vice, for the sake of his Estates, & disbelieving any
would accept him for any other reason. He wrongs
both Them & Himself by this conclusion.

And, heck, that sorta sounds like love to me.

I mean, not that I would know, of course. Spinsters are not generally considered to be the very best
authorities on love. It's not one of our historical areas
of expertise. Like, say, embroidering things. Or writing novels. Or securing the vote. But it *does* seem to
me that if you need that many adjectives to describe a
person, *something* must be going on. And indeed, in all
of Fanny's many encounters with Jeremiah Crutchley,
she always seems to be *moved* by him in some essential
way:

He makes her mad.

He makes her sad.

He makes her sorry to see him wretched beyond
measure.

Very often, when she re-creates their dialogues, she
describes him as "laughing."

Or sometimes "half laughing."

Or sometimes *she's* laughing.

At a really bad haircut he's just gotten.

At something saucily sarcastic he's just said to Mrs.
Thrale.

Or sometimes at something saucily sarcastic he's

just said to *her*—for as Fanny herself once put it…

FANNY

```
He makes less ceremony with me
than any man I ever knew.
```

And she backs this up with examples:
"Nonsense" (spelled with a "c" passes among them).
"Teizing" takes place.
Merriment is had.
But it wasn't all good times.

Jeremiah Crutchley was also, by her own admission, the first man Fanny ever *quarreled* with, and if you've ever seen a typical, by-the-numbers Hollywood romantic comedy or tried to write one or read any books that purport to tell you all the rules of how to write one—well, then you basically know what that means…

It means you're in love but you just don't know it yet.

Of course, a lot of people tend to think that is bullshit. They think it's impossible to be in love without *knowing* you're in love, and I don't know if this is consequence or coincidence, but those people tend to be the same people who can't stand romantic comedies. They get bored watching people bumbling around for two hours when it's totally obvious from the get-go who's in love with whom, and they'd probably get even more bored if they were forced to watch a six-part miniseries about a nearsighted, badly dressed novelist who never has any idea who she's in love with. Although I tend to think that if it's the summer of 1781, and you haven't been exposed to a lot of popular entertainment on the subject of Love—you know, apart from the popular entertainment that you yourself have written on the subject—well, in that case I think people should cut you a little slack and agree that it's possible to be in love without actually knowing you're in love.

Mrs. Thrale, Fanny's best friend, agreed with me on this point. In September 1781, she wrote in her diary, "I think She honestly loves the Man," and reading that, I'm sold. I don't need to stop and gather any more evidence because in my world (the world of teenage melodrama), that sort of declaration carries a lot of weight. An avowal of love from a best friend? Heck, in certain situations—depending on where it takes place and to whom it's being avowed—that could even be, like, a second-act break or something. Because in the world of teenage melodrama, if your best friend says that you love someone—guess what?

You probably do.

But I guess people who write *scholarly* biographies need more evidence than that. They can't just go around creating act breaks and rewriting history based on something some BFF wrote in her diary. They have to stick to the facts—just the facts—which is where Fanny's lifelong habit of Journaling for Anxiety™ should absolutely positively totally come in handy. Only here's the rub: the pages of Fanny's diary that might actually explain what the fuck was going on with her and Jeremiah Crutchley during the summer of 1781—the part when she comes to "relate the conclusion of Mr. Crutchly's [sic] most extraordinary summer career at Streatham"—well, those pages seem to be missing.

They're gone.

They've been lost to history.

Either Fanny destroyed them because she didn't want future generations to know the conclusion of "Mr. Crutchly's [sic] most extraordinary summer career at Streatham," or the person who inherited all of Fanny's diaries and letters—her niece, Charlotte Barrett—destroyed them because *she* didn't want people to know, or somebody just spilled something on them and they got all fucked up.

It's been a long time since 1781.

Shit happens.

I get that. But obviously, this is a major bummer from the perspective of someone who has gotten herself all emotionally involved with Jeremiah Crutchley and devoted an entire episode of her six-part miniseries to him. The Thomas Barlow Affair (aka Part One of my six-part miniseries) has a really great ending: She says no, she refuses to marry him, she chooses The Spinster Way—fade out, cut to commercial, end of episode. The George Owen Cambridge saga in Part Three will also have a satisfying conclusion. Or, wait, maybe it won't be satisfying. Maybe it'll just be heartbreaking. But to have no ending? To be left hanging like this, to never know what actually went down between Jeremiah Crutchley and Fanny Burney during the summer of 1781? For a storyteller, a *professional* storyteller, to do that to her audience—well, I always hate to judge Fanny, I hate to harsh on her, but that just seems cruel, don't you think? Cruel and unusual. No, when I finally get unstuck and make it back to that incident in Part Two of my ill-fated, six-part miniseries, I'll do what any self-respecting member of the Writers Guild would do...

I'll lie.

I'll lay it on thick about how Jeremiah Crutchley actually really did love Fanny Burney. I'll say he was totally into her, thought she was amazing, couldn't get enough of her. I'll say it didn't bother him that she was a successful, hardworking novelist prone to lurking fevers. If I'm making shit up, why not, right? Why not just toss Fanny that tiny little bone. The woman's going to live to be eighty-seven, for Chrissake. She's got *tons* of heartbreak ahead of her; a lot of bad times. Like in early 1800, her favorite sister, Susanna—the one who loved to play the piano and spoke French really well—is going to die in lodgings in a town called Parkgate. That's totally going to break Fanny's heart. And then in 1811, when she's fifty-nine, she's going to get breast cancer, and they're going to cut off her right breast... *without anesthesia.*

Not great, right? But in the summer of 1781, things

are still going pretty well for Fanny. She's in the midst of trying to write her second chick-lit novel, *Cecilia; Or, Memoirs of an Heiress.* The goddamn thing is like a thousand pages long, so Fanny will *still* be trying to write it in the fall of 1781, the winter of 1781, that next spring, etc., etc., &c. Basically, Fanny will be writing *Cecilia* right up until the very moment it goes to press in June 1782, and it ends up being a ridiculously huge success. Princesses will read it. Dowager duchesses. Milliners. Bishops. Members of Parliaments. It won't make her tons of money or dramatically improve her love life, but at least it will be done. Finished. Over. At which point, things will begin to go drastically downhill for Fanny. Parts Three, Four, and Five of my miniseries? I don't want to give too much away, but those next ten years are going to be kind of tough for my heroine—kind of sucky. That whole *mishegoss* with George Owen Cambridge is really going to take it out of her, and that job she gets working for the Queen? Ugh. Double ugh. *That* job.

No way would I ever wish that job on my worst enemy, so before things start to suck so completely for Fanny, I think it might be nice—both for her and for the overall dramaturgical flow of the ill-fated, six-part miniseries—to pause for just a brief moment and let this one tiny little thing go her way. Lord knows you can't have the real-estate-based happily-ever-after at the end of Part Two of your ill-fated, six-part miniseries (even

I'm not that crazy), but there's no reason you can't have a little summer romance. Nonsense! Teizing! Even a few moonlit walks. Something lighthearted, carefree, breezy, optimistic—something filled with hope. That's where the hope goes, right? In Part Two, when you're twenty-nine. Twenty-nine is the age of hope, the last moment where everything seems possible. That's the way I'm writing Part Two of my ill-fated, six-part mini-series. Also, it would annoy me too goddamn much to write the version where what was really going on that summer was that Jeremiah Crutchley was actually in love with Mrs. Thrale.

Or with Mrs. Thrale's seventeen-year-old daughter.

Those are the other two, very real historical possibilities that totally explain what the fuck Jeremiah Crutchley was doing hanging out all the damn time at Mrs. Thrale's country house, and if you think about things calmly and logically, they do make tons of sense.

Mrs. Thrale was famously beautiful, totally not shy, and had loads of money.

Plus, she was only four years older than Crutchley, which isn't many if you think about it. Her daughter was—well, her daughter was seventeen. And that's another way in which the world hasn't changed much since the late eighteenth century. Seems to me if you take a wealthy thirty-six-year-old guy of *any* century and give him a choice between a timid, twenty-nine-year-old novelist, a sexy-dangerous widow of forty, and the widow's seventeen-year-old daughter—more often than not, no matter what century he's from, he's gonna choose the seventeen-year-old girl.

But, frankly, I don't really see the fun in telling that story. Agents love to sell it. Cable networks love to buy it. But don't most of us know it already? Also, the story about the "empowered," sexy, older woman, the rich widow who's been doing Pilates and looks great and therefore has her pick of suitors—that one sounds kind of familiar too, right? That one's not *unprecedented*. But the story about the thirty-six-year-old guy who falls in love with the widow's timid, impoverished best friend? That's the one we haven't heard before, right? Rarely in contemporary, twenty-first-century LA do a bunch of entertainment professionals get together and decide to tell a story about anything happening to anyone's best friend. We have laws against that here. And we certainly don't ever get together and tell a *love* story about the Best Friend. No, mostly we just keep the Best Friend around so that the Main Character has someone to talk to about her love-related difficulties. Maybe we cast an acerbic chubby girl with glasses. Or a gay guy unafraid to walk around in culottes. Either way, the Best Friend basically doesn't have to do anything except listen to all the Main Character's bullshit and act all sympathetic about it, which is *exactly* what Fanny ultimately ended up doing for Mrs. Thrale in real life.

Yes, it's true.

Three summers later, Mrs. Thrale actually ran off to Italy and married her daughter's music teacher. This caused a scandal *so* big that Dr. Johnson had a stroke, lost the power of speech, and *died* over it, only I don't have time to get into that right now because of my new plan to submit Part One of my ill-fated miniseries to the BBC—write up a proposal, do a synopsis of all the episodes, etc., etc., &c. Also, any second now, the people who hired me to work on this television show are going to figure to out that they're paying me huge sums of money to sit in my office all day Journaling for Anxiety™ and sorting out eighteenth-century love quadrangles, and then they're going to give me another writing assignment.

Or make me go back in the story room.

I can just feel it. I've been in the network-TV writing game long enough to have a sixth sense about when some giant shitstorm of revisions is about to hit. Somewhere behind closed doors, at least one episode must be going down. Maybe two? Seriously. It's far too quiet around here. This doesn't bode well for the rest of the year.

Or the rest of the week.

THURSDAY, NOVEMBER 23, 2006

WELL, I'VE DONE IT.

I've made it all the way to Thanksgiving.

Which is both the beginning and the end of *Hannah and Her Sisters*. Only this Thanksgiving hasn't wound up being at all like either of those two, where Carrie Fisher cracks wise and old people sing songs around a piano.

No, this Thanksgiving (like all my Thanksgivings) wound up being a lot more like that part in *Annie Hall* where the screen splits and we see everyone in Alvie's family shoving food into their mouths and shouting at each other about which family members have various ailments: diabetes, a coronary. I honestly don't know why I keep making these weird little holiday jaunts back to the Rust Belt. They never seem to go too well. I always end up catching some kind of pestilence from my six nieces and nephews or getting food poisoning or a migraine or nearly fainting in the three-hour line to pick up a rental car at O'Hare.

Thank god for other spinsters traveling alone who will offer to watch your stuff while you go to the vending machine to buy some pretzels.

No, the sad truth that must be faced here is that I have failed—completely and utterly failed—in my original mission to combine my brain tumor with a stressed-out, overworked TV-writing career and produce a frothy little *Hannah and Her Sisters*–inspired romantic comedy.

Witty banter.

Great clothes.

Love Interests, both true and faux.

You've simply *got* to have that stuff in a romantic comedy, and because of my devotion to The Spinster Way, I can't bring any of that to the table. Jill actually pointed this out the other day. In a nice way, but still she noticed it. She said that back in June when she first met me, she expected me to be like the shoe girls and have some sort of *story* I desperately needed to tell about my singleness—about why my "relationships" never work out, or about how surprised I am to have ended up here over thirty and, alas, still single. But after about five months of lunches, she said it started to dawn on her that I wasn't just being shy or holding back all my super boring, sexually explicit stories out of some exaggerated sense of propriety.

And she's right.

I really don't have any stories like that to tell. Not a one. So instead I seem to be borrowing Fanny's…

Thomas Barlow.

Jeremiah Crutchley.

George Owen Cambridge.

Hell, I've even left some out just to speed things along. Sir Joshua Reynolds. Heard of him? Super famous portrait painter. Mostly deaf and nearly thirty years older than Fanny. I swear there's a point in the diaries where he comes up as a possible suitor. A slightly more age-appropriate option was Fanny's very young, handsome cousin, Edward Francisco Burney, who painted her portrait not once, but twice.

But then again, he might have been *too* young and handsome.

After all, we tend not to like it so much when a romantic comedy heroine is nearly a decade *older* than the Love Interest. That never really goes over well at the box office. Still, family legend always had it that Edward had a thing for Fanny, and the main way he seems to have expressed this thing is by refusing to go for long walks and leaning against the chimney doing nothing, which—in my humble opinion—isn't really all that different from how the young people of today express their love-related inclinations.

Certainly, if you spend any time during the doldrums of October talking to the twentysomething assistants about their love lives, the concept of immobility always seems to creep into the conversation at some point. Dave, for instance, has tons of stories like this to tell. They never involve leaning against a chimney—there's usually some modern equivalent, like lying on the couch watching *Rocky V*—but the effect is basically the same. And he's not even in his twenties anymore. Nope, he's definitely made the leap into his early thirties, which I had begun to suspect based on his cultural references; and now it's been confirmed because we had one of those wretched office birthdays for him, and he owned up to being thirty-two. The other thing that's been confirmed about Dave—and it pains me to say this, because this is *way* worse of a crime than being over thirty and still working as a writers' assistant, or wearing flip-flops every day when it's November and there's fake snow all over the lot—well, it turns out that Dave, our very own Dave, is one of the Wishy-Washy.

You see, he lives with this girlfriend he's always going on about (the one who knows some of the same people I know), and I suppose it could be really sweet that he's always going on about her, except that *specifically* what he's always going on about is how much he wants to break up with this girl. Only he can't, because she's so nice, they've been together for years now, how would he ever find another girl who was better than this one, etc., etc., &c.

Textbook Wishy-Washy, no?

They're the scourge of the twenty-first century, the Wishy-Washy, in exactly the same way that Rakes were once the scourge of the eighteenth century, but can I be honest here?

They're not a terribly interesting scourge.

Rakes had style; they had panache. They drove a low-hung curricle. They ran off to Gretna Green with your sister. They did stuff—and they did it in a timely manner. The Wishy-Washy tend to inflict the majority of their damage by *not* doing things.

They don't call.

They don't say I love you.

They don't propose.

They do nothing and they say nothing, and in many instances they will actually drag out this doing-and-saying-nothing process for *years* before they decide to move on and do nothing and say nothing with a different girl. Although maybe I shouldn't use the word "girl" quite so freely, because Jill—using her amazing, married-lady powers of inquisition—pulled it out of Dave that the girl in question, the one he admits he *definitely* doesn't want to settle down and have children with, well, it turns out this girl is almost forty.

That's right.

She's quite a bit *older* than Dave is, which instantly shed a whole new light on the Dave situation, because before, I guess we all thought he was wasting the prime childbearing years of a girl in her *early* thirties, but now we realize he's doing this to a girl her late thirties, and even though he does seem to be *aware* that this is a pretty shitty thing to do to someone, still, it bears repeating.

So Jill repeated it.

In what I *swear* was a very nice way.

And then eventually, we got back to discussing the personal lives of the characters on the show.

We've been doing a lot more of that lately.

Staying in the room for hours and hours. Working through lunch. Ordering pizza at night. Rebreaking stories that have already been broken and written and prepped and cast, and then at the last second, someone will have a freak-out about one of them, and it will have to be reconfigured in some huge way that makes it *seem* different to the actors and the network, but still uses all the standing sets in a cost-efficient manner. It's confusing, I know, but it's just how things work in TV. Obviously, it's way more fun to sit around talking about the personal lives of the people in the room. That's how interesting revelations come to light, like this one about Dave being one of the Wishy-Washy and wasting the prime childbearing years of an unsuspecting female who probably shouldn't be so unsuspecting, and even though I now have a brand-new writing assignment to obsess over—Jill and I are going to cowrite Episode 16!—and all hell is breaking loose in the story room, I feel I would be remiss if I did not take a moment to point that this is exactly, and I do mean exactly, what happened with Fanny and that evil bastard of a clergyman George Owen Cambridge.

In her early thirties, the not-so-young Miss Frances Burney made what may have been the biggest mistake of her life. She put all her eggs in a basket marked

George Owen Cambridge, and I think we can all guess how that turned out. Sounds familiar, right? Everybody knows that girl. She's among the legions of females walking around today who spent their prime childbearing years "hanging out" in a wide variety of nonspecific, non-legally-binding ways with some guy who never produced a ring, and now they are all old and expired and, alas, *still single*.

Well, back in Fanny's day, this was not the usual order of business. Nope, back then people knew exactly how dangerous "hanging out" could be. How often it led to heartache, and, more significantly, in a patriarchal society plagued by a lack of effective birth control methods, unwanted pregnancy and the nagging fear that your eldest son wasn't really your eldest son. So back then, if you were a guy who enjoyed *hanging out* with a girl—if you found her interesting or sweet or kind or ridiculously beautiful or basically your parents just really enjoyed the fact that she was totally loaded—well, at a certain point you were required to *declare your intentions*.

This was not negotiable.

You had to state, unequivocally, what exactly you were prepared to do about the situation, and while I'm sure that was a major bummer for the guys of the past—you know, having to be all decisive and shit—in exchange for this onerous burden, they got to vote and own property and do tons of stuff adult women of the late eighteenth century couldn't even begin to think about doing, like wearing pants and leaving the house unchaperoned.

And this is basically where Fanny got into trouble with George Owen Cambridge.

They saw each other eight times between December 26, 1782, and January 18, 1783.

Eight times in four weeks.

That feels like a lot, no?

Fanny's BFF Mrs. Thrale seemed to think so.

By February 1783, she was teasing Fanny: "Is George Cambridge in love with you, or is he not?" And in April, she writes more definitively: "My dearest Miss Burney has apparently got an Admirer in Mr George Cambridge." And then she goes on to say, "If they marry, I shall have perhaps more of her Company than now, for her Mother in Law [i.e., her Wicked Stepmother] is a greater Tyrant than any Husband would be, especially a Man whose heart is apparently engaged."

The key word here being "apparently."

Remember George Owen Cambridge was one of a new breed of men.

He wasn't a Rake.

He wasn't a Nice Guy.

He was one of the Wishy-Washy.

And back in the late eighteenth century, the Wishy-Washy approach to courtship was so novel, so revolutionary, so utterly new, that no one quite knew what to make of it. It flummoxed everyone—old, young, men, women—which, now that I think about it, probably explains why Fanny got such shitty advice about her love life during this time. Her contemporaries just couldn't parse it. It didn't compute. Why would a man spend so much time *hanging out* with a woman he had no intention of marrying?

It seemed like love, this elaborate game George Owen Cambridge was playing. It seemed like courtship. It certainly followed all the *rules* of courtship, and even some of the Rules for Romantic Comedy.

He sat next to her at parties.

He stopped by the house on St. Martin's Street.

He shared private jokes with her about Mrs. Vesey's hearing aid.

He was incredibly nice to her gay best friend.

Or, you know, since they didn't officially have gay people back then, her best Italian-castrato-singer friend.

Eventually, Fanny's favorite sister, Susanna (the one who loved to play the piano and spoke French really well), was able to get to the bottom of this perplexing behavior. Of course, by that point, Fanny had lost all her career momentum and her prime childbearing years were disappearing in the rearview mirror—but, hey, we have to cut the favorite sister some slack. Back in 1782, she married an officer in the Royal Marines named Molesworth Phillips, and by 1785 she had two small children and some sort of serious health problem that required her to move to France for a year. Plus, this Molesworth Phillips character turned out to be a gambler and an unfeeling reprobate, which will come up big-time in Part Five of my six-part miniseries, but once again I am getting away from the point, which is that eventually, Fanny's favorite sister did what no one else walking around Georgian England could do circa 1786.

She figured out what the friggin' deal was with George Owen Cambridge. She classified it. She gave it a name. She decided he meant to be a "particular & intimate friend, yet no more."

Or as we would say in modern parlance: *he just wasn't that into her.*

∾

Crushes happen. They do. They happen to the best of us. Sometimes I think I might actually be having one now, but I'm thirty-eight years old and I know better than that, so I fight it. I resist. After all, a crush is like an orchid: it has to be cultivated. It has to have water and light and special plant food and god knows what else to survive. Emotional encouragement, perhaps. They're delicate things, crushes. Katie, the delightful twentysomething assistant-girl who brings me a double tall cappuccino every afternoon, has one right now. It's on the guy who delivers the copier paper, and we have all, as an office, rallied together and become invested in this crush. We ask her questions about it, detain the poor guy in banal conversations, send her on pointless errands to his end of the lot. The shoe girls will even sit Katie down from time to time and dispense sage advice on how she should go about transforming the crush into something real—although I tend not to participate so much in this part of the process, because one of the many important life lessons I have learned from my decades-long obsessive study of the fortunes and misfortunes of the famous Miss Burney is that nothing good ever comes from a crush.

Or wait, shit—that's not entirely true.

I once got a job from a crush.

In the spring of 1994—a simpler time, if ever there was one—I had an obsessive crush on the goateed latte guy who worked at my local Starbucks. Since there weren't any shoe girls around to give me well-meaning advice—shoe girls didn't actually exist yet circa 1994—I didn't put on makeup and a sexy outfit and attempt to "accidentally" run into him at different places around town. Instead, I wrote a *story* about the obsessive crush, and then I sent that story to my local alternative newspaper, and they gave me a check for $267 and a job as an assistant editor. And even though it was a little embarrassing when they published the story and the goateed latte guy found out I had an obsessive crush on him, and after that everybody kinda pointed and stared at me whenever I went into the Starbucks on Diversey—still, that *job* was a good thing.

It kept me fed and clothed and paid for my teeny-tiny studio apartment on Sheridan Road, and everybody else who worked at the alternative newspaper seemed to be reading the same books I was reading, and every once in a while I would get to go to a concert for free with one of the rock critics; and probably if I had never gotten The Phone Call That Changed My Life and packed up and moved all my writerly dreams to LA, I would still be living in that teeny-tiny studio apartment on Sheridan Road and working at the alternative newspaper and trying in vain every week to get the rock critics to listen to me about where the semicolons should go.

So technically speaking, you could say that crush changed my life for the better.

But not every crush ends so happily.

Fanny's certainly didn't. Which is why, at this point in our saga, it starts to be a good thing that the im-poverished academics who make it their life's work to edit the official, unabridged version of Fanny's diaries and letters haven't reached 1783 yet. Apparently they're quite painful to read—all the sad, crazy bits of Fanny's diary where the most successful female novelist on the planet goes on and on in lots of angst-ridden, excru-ciating detail about the not-so-fascinating subject of whether some douchebag clergyman likes her or not.

That's what Frances Burney, Mother of English Fiction, wrote during the years 1783 to 1786.

And that's all she wrote.

Instead of following up her first two phenomenally successful chick-lit novels with a third phenomenally successful chick-lit novel—which, hello, any self-respecting literary agent would totally advise a person to do—instead of honing her craft and grasping for the higher sort of literary immortality achieved one short generation later by a clergyman's daughter named Jane, Frances Burney, in her early thirties, took a break from the arduous, fever-inducing task of writing novels and devoted herself exclusively to Journaling for Anxiety™.

Interesting career choice, no?

And even though she knew how this whole wretched episode turned out—even though she knew that in the end, George Owen Cambridge *wasn't* that into her, that he didn't love her back, that they would *not* live happily ever after—still, she kept all the evidence of her angsting and obsessing around.

She didn't toss it or torch it or whatever.

She lugged it around with her from 1786 till she died in 1840, to and from all her various jobs and lodgings and so forth.

And then she bequeathed it all to her niece Charlotte Barrett, and luckily *she* didn't torch or trash it, and nowadays it's all stashed away for posterity in the research collections of the New York Public Library.

Which is where I used to work right after I graduated from the less-famous Ivy League university I attended.

Sort of a funny coincidence, no?

Only back then, I was not so inordinately obsessed with Frances Burney. Her troubles, her times, her romantic difficulties, these things didn't preoccupy me so much. I'm not sure what did. A logical guess would be my own romantic difficulties, but I swear I was a spinster back then, too—I've *always* been a spinster—so I didn't really have any of those.

Or if I had them, I guess I didn't *realize* I had them.

Like sometimes, I would have these odd work-related encounters I couldn't quite parse—Israeli art dealers would tell me they liked the sound of my voice on the phone, or restaurateurs would give me their business cards at fancy charity events, or the waiters at the fancy charity events would try to engage me in conversations about the class struggle—and it would always have to be explained to me after the fact that the guys in these scenarios had been trying to hit on me. But it's not like life ever throws you back into the paths of those exact same cater waiters or restaurateurs or Israeli art dealers, so I guess I never really got a chance to rectify those mistakes.

If they actually were mistakes.

Either way, I apologize to them all—to all the guys who lived in New York in the early nineties and may or may not have tried to hit on me at various points. I'm sure a lot of them were really nice, especially the one who wanted to talk about the class struggle. I just didn't see it at the time. Not because they weren't good-looking enough or because I was holding out for guys with more glorified jobs than cater waiter or whatever. It's just that it had always been repeatedly drilled into my head during my formative years that boys would only like me if I looked a certain way—a distinctly thin, non-glasses-wearing, non-spinsterish way—and even though I can look back now, in retrospect, and see that when I was in my early twenties I wasn't really all that bad-looking, still, it never really occurred to me back then that I looked okay enough to go on dates or have a boyfriend or try to be the heroine of my very own romantic comedy the way the shoe girls seem to be doing.

So perhaps *that's* what I was obsessing on?

How un-normal I looked?

Obviously, it hadn't yet occurred to me that I should stop obsessing on myself and my many flaws and devote myself to the arduous task of constructing a six-part miniseries documenting the career struggles and romantic difficulties of Frances Burney, Mother of English Fiction. I guess that's why it never occurred to me, back then, that I should march upstairs and ask the research librarians if I could please look at all of Fanny Burney's super sad eighteenth-century Journaling for Anxiety™.

No way I'm doing that now, though. Putting on white gloves, searching through archives? Not my cup of tea. Oh, I'm sure I'll read all that stuff when it finally does come out, professionally edited and footnoted and such. I owe it to Fanny—heck, I owe it to my six-part miniseries—but in all honestly, it seems like it's going to be a major bummer.

You know, watching someone who's been one of the Top Five Heroes of My Life lose her shit and destroy her career over some douchebag clergyman who just wasn't that into her.

You know the drill.

Like I said before, this is a huge problem we have here in modern times: guys and girls are always *hanging out* together—going to movies, having sex, even buying furniture—without ever specifically defining what their hanging out means. And we certainly don't have any laws or rules etched in stone about how, after a certain point, the guys in these scenarios should just get their shit together and decide they're done with one girl and ready to move on to the next one. Although I would like to take a brief moment to suggest that *if we did*, I think we could cut down on a lot of the workplace crying that so hinders our productivity as a nation. I think some government agency might want to look into that. You know, for efficiency's sake.

In Fanny's day, of course, they did have those kinds of rules. Zillions of them. But for some strange reason, when it came to Fanny, George Owen Cambridge didn't see fit to follow any of them.

Perhaps he assumed the rules didn't apply to novelist-girls.

Or celebrities.

Or girls whose fathers were music teachers. Remember, Fanny had no money and no impressive family connections. Her father was a social butterfly and a hell of a piano player, but he was not the kind of guy who would take you out behind the Bada Bing and beat some sense into you if your courtship of his daughter deviated from the social norm into some vague, uncharted territory that wouldn't really have a name until a novelist named Fielding, near the close of the twentieth century, coined the term "emotional fuckwittage."

Of course, it's also possible that the whole thing may have been Fanny's fault.

Yes, maybe that's it. I'm always protecting her, taking her side. But perhaps she was the one who fucked the whole thing up. Perhaps she was too guarded in her affections. Too reserved. Too, you know…*spinsterish*. Maybe Fanny could have landed George Owen Cambridge if she'd acted more like the shoe girls—been a little less timid and more flirtatious. Done more to "fix him," as they would have said back then, meaning, you know, to nail him down, secure his affections, get the ring. Although, wait, I just realized, we still use that expression, don't we? We still talk all the time about girls "fixing" guys, only nowadays we mean getting them to dress better and not watch so much football; back then it seems to have meant something more akin to "affixing" them. You know, getting them stuck on you.

Either way, time kept ticking—1783 turned into 1784, into 1785, into 1786—and George Cambridge Owen didn't propose.

But he also didn't go away.

He just kept sitting next to Fanny at parties and making everybody who knew them *think* he was going to propose, and so at the age of thirty-four, she did the only thing a super successful female writer could do, circa 1786, if she wasn't getting any younger, she wasn't descended from a long line of rich people, and no gentleman of means particularly wanted to marry her: she took a really prestigious, well-paying job that was super hard to get, and everybody who knew her thought it would be really glamorous and great, but guess what?

It wasn't.

It was just like every other shitty job on the planet.

To-Do List

- Ideas for Episode 16, coordinate with Jill
- Submit proposal to BBC, finish part one, write summaries of episodes, etc., etc., &c.
- Plane ticket for Xmas
- ~~Pick Up Dry Cleaning~~
- Decide When to Have Brain Surgery
- Read Dave's Spec Script

SATURDAY, DECEMBER 16, 2006

TODAY AT THE GYM it was just me and Anorexic Unabomber Girl.

Which kinda makes me question my lifestyle choices.

Because even though working all day on your outline and then doing 3.53 miles on the elliptical trainer sounds like a vaguely healthy way to spend a Saturday, it doesn't necessarily seem so healthy when the only other person doing it with you is a skeletal, Death-like apparition of a girl wearing the world's largest, bulkiest hooded sweatshirt with the hood pulled way down over her face and multiple towels thrown over her neck, as if she's a boxer in a 1930s movie.

Also, the headaches have gotten worse.

But if you ask me, that's got nothing to do with the brain tumor.

No, in my humble opinion, the headaches have gotten worse because we're officially in high-drama mode *all the time* now at the office, and to make matters worse, the dreaded "holiday" season is upon us. You know, that oh-so-special time of year when presents and plane tickets must be purchased and parties attended and everyone—not just the ladies who are over thirty and still single, but *everyone*—wakes up every day wanting to off themselves. There just isn't any time between Thanksgiving and Christmas, is there? It's like you blink and it's gone. But the good news is that I am invited to a festive holiday party tonight at the home of a friend who's way more successful in the entertainment industry than I am, and the main reason this qualifies as good news is that it gave me something to say all week when people at work asked me...

COWORKER
Any plans for the weekend?

Like just now, when Jill sent me an email checking in about how my half of our outline was going, I was able to respond with some cheerful, vaguely normal-sounding info about how I was just about to stop working and go to a party in the Hollywood Hills, which is true.

I'm totally going to go.

I've got an outfit picked out and everything. It involves a new skirt I got off the sale rack at Banana Republic, and even though it might not be much by shoe-girl standards, I really would like to have some-place to wear this skirt. Plus, I already told my friend Jay I was going, and I don't want to let him down, and, heck, at this point, it would be kind of silly *not* to go, because if I stay home and blow the whole thing off to watch some spinster classic I've already seen ten thousand times like *Summertime*—well, then obviously I won't have anything to say when people ask me on Monday...

Do anything fun this weekend?

So probably I'll just go.

I should, right? Just for appearances' sake. It's not like the party itself promises to be such a life-changing good time. I can already tell you in advance just exactly what the evening will be like. Lots of gay men will come up and talk to me. They will find me literate and charming and funny, and if I'm lucky—god willing, fingers crossed—I'll get out of there without agreeing to read anyone's spec script.

That would be my definition of a great Saturday night: leave the house, talk to someone a little more gregarious than Anorexic Unabomber Girl, and return home without any additional spec scripts I've promised to read. Dave gave me his way back in early November, and when I got back from Thanksgiving, I finally read it and sent him some notes over email. It seemed easier than having an entire conversation with him about it face-to-face. Not that we would have time for that anyway. No, right now Jill and I are in a desperate rush to finish the outline for our new episode and get it approved before December 20, when all the execs leave for Christmas vacation. That way, we'll be able to spend our Christmas vacations writing. Plus, somehow I agreed to be the person who takes care of arranging cash bonuses for the assistants and getting a Christmas present for our boss, which really isn't such a big deal because one of the shoe girls already came up with a funny idea about what to get him, so now all I have to do is go pick it up at Nordstrom. I kinda hate to admit this, but it is actually pretty funny.

Shoes.

You know, because of the shoe contest, which is now officially over, BTW.

The girl with the most shoes won.

SATURDAY, JANUARY 27, 2007

HELLO! Is ANYBODY out there reading this? If you are, I am probably dead. Is there a preface you skipped? Some sort of foreword written by a PhD or a learned physician? Go back and check. If there's a foreword, I probably am dead, and the cosmic joke of it all is that it wasn't even the brain tumor that killed me. That would be hilarious, wouldn't it? Here I spend all these months Journaling for Anxiety™ and obsessing like a crazy person on my brain tumor—is it getting bigger, is it changing my personality, should I get it taken out?—and then what gets me in the end *isn't* the head thing. It's the other thing: the sex thing, the gynecological thing.

'Cause that would be really funny, right?

To be a spinster and live a life virtually devoid of sexual shenanigans and then *die* from some embarrassing gynecological ailment that you can't even talk about with your coworkers, except for Jill, who thinks it would be totally okay if I left work in the middle of the day next Friday to go have this weird, highly unpleasant-sounding test I'm supposed to have now that my gynecologist has found something else wrong with me?

That's right.

With my brain tumor in a holding pattern, I went in for yet another routine ultrasound on my fibroid, and a *third* abnormal thing came up—a third "finding"

I have to keep track of and get scanned and drive to Beverly Hills and watch and wait and worry about. To be honest, I'm not really sure what this latest medical plot twist is all about. It started yesterday when the gyno left me a message on my home machine saying my last ultrasound was abnormal and that I should schedule this additional test, and there didn't seem to be any point in calling her back and trying to get additional info because:

a) her office is incredibly disorganized,

b) they keep you on hold for centuries, and

c) there's not really any part of this that isn't totally upsetting and scary.

Apparently, what's wrong with me now has something to do with "thick endometrial lining," and when I Googled that, I got the sort of awful, terrifying stuff that I didn't get the first time around when I Googled my brain tumor—i.e., cancer. And then when I called the radiology place to schedule the test, they didn't even bother to *pretend* that the test would be totally easy and painless.

You know, like medical professionals so often do.

Nope, the person on the phone admitted flat-out that this particular test was incredibly unpleasant and then she actually told me to take Advil before I came in to prepare for how unpleasant it would be. So there's really no way to REMAIN CALM ABOUT THIS and spin the whole thing positively like I did last January when my charming, Omar Sharif–like ear, nose, and throat doctor called on Friday the 13th and told me I had a small brain tumor pressing on my frontal lobe.

So how about you, dear reader, if you're out there? Did you have a good Christmas?

I can't say I did. In fact, it's basically been one long, nonstop river of sadness around here since we started back after New Year's. One night last week, we actually had to stay late and open a bottle of Dom because one of the shoe girls got her pilot picked up, and even though drinking expensive French Champagne and making awkward chitchat with your coworkers doesn't in and of itself *sound* sad, somehow it took everything I had not to burst into tears during this ritual. I'm not quite sure why. Maybe I should make a list? Top Five Reasons I Might Be Sad? It was before I got the abnormal test results back, so it can't be that. I guess I must be jealous, right? Yes, that must be it. I must be jealous that my pilot didn't get picked up, although the big problem with that theory is that I don't even have a pilot. I had one last year, but like most pilots, it didn't get picked up, so instead I picked myself up, brushed myself off, and started writing a typical, by-the-numbers, Hollywood romantic comedy screenplay, and then a few days after that, I found out I had a small brain tumor pressing on my frontal lobe, and I can't say that I've thought much about it since then.

My pilot, I mean.

Obviously, I've thought a lot about my brain tumor.

From this I suppose we could deduce that having a subfrontal midline meningioma pressing on your olfactory nerve is an excellent way to get over any lingering sadness you might have about your pilot not getting picked up. It's sort of like Prozac in that regard.

Not that I, personally, had any sadness.

Maybe I'm kidding myself about this—maybe I'm in denial and whatnot—but when I look back at that time, I think I was more sad *while* I was getting network notes and writing the seventeenth draft of my pilot than I was after I found out that my pilot wasn't going to be picked up and shot and possibly turned into a TV show. I certainly didn't throw up or have any strange, unexplained vertigo incidents *after* I found out my pilot was dead. Nope, all those weird medical things happened *before*, back in the days when my pilot was still alive. So maybe it was *sadness* that made me throw up in the private bathroom of my giant office at Sunset/Gower studios and go running to my charming, Omar Sharif–like ENT? I suppose that could be it, right? Maybe sadness works that way? More likely, it was just bad sushi. Frankly, I never really trusted that place next to the Bed Bath & Beyond, and I haven't been back there since.

Shit, can you believe it's been a whole year since then?

Exactly one year since my pilot didn't get picked up and I inadvertently discovered I had a benign brain tumor. That's the great part about having a brain tumor. If you have a brain tumor, they will actually call and tell you have a brain tumor.

But if you don't, they will also call and tell you you're fine.

You're okay.

Everything's good.

That's the call you want to get in any type of tumor-related situation. It's the one I wanted to get yesterday, but instead I got the call where they tell you something is abnormal and you have to come back for a second, more horrifying and painful test that requires taking Advil beforehand, which shouldn't be a problem for me because I have basically been taking Advil every day since Christmas.

Like, remember those headaches that I thought were getting worse back in December?

Well, they're basically happening every day now.

At least the script went fine, the one I was doing with Jill. Filming started yesterday, so it's all behind me now, and there's no possible need to worry about it anymore. Episode 16, done. Crossed off my list of Things To Do. It is what it is. Certain things I wrote got rewritten; others did not. And for the first time in my career, I think I finally realized that there is absolutely no correlation between how much effort and mental anguish I put into writing the script I have been assigned and the result that comes out the other side. It's sort of counterintuitive in a way, this idea that no matter how hard you work, you will never get any better at your job, and I guess that's why it's taken me eight years of moderately successful TV writing to figure it out and see it so clearly. The process is just too random, too arbitrary. It's all governed by caprice—the whims of actors, the whims of showrunners, the whims of networks—so even though being rewritten is an incredibly unpleasant sensation that evokes feelings of failure and shame and makes you feel like you are a rat in one of those experiments where the rats get shocked with an electrode every time they do something wrong and that's how you demonstrate that rats can learn things—well, when you're a moderately successful TV writer, you're not really that rat.

You're actually a different rat.

You're like this special Hollywood rat who gets shocked with an electrode at totally random times that have nothing to do with anything, and that's how you demonstrate that rats really *can't* learn things. No, even if you pay them tons of money and give them great parking spaces, when you shock them with electrodes day in and day out, they just get really confused, hopeless, and depressed and lose all connection to their original instincts. And that's why it takes the rats eight long years of moderately successful TV writing to figure out that all the effort and mental anguish they're putting into *analyzing* the system that supplies all these unpleasant shocks is completely wasted.

Of course, in order to have this particular aha moment, you have to be able to see yourself as some type of lab animal. If not a rat, then at least a dog, like one of Pavlov's. Or possibly, if you're wearing $500 shoes and feeling really glamorous, a monkey. Because at least monkeys, like overpaid TV writers, have language—rudimentary language, yes, but language nonetheless. Either way, you're totally powerless and insignificant (and guess what, hello, you live in a cage), and nobody in Hollywood likes that feeling. That's why we put names on the parking spaces and give everyone nice offices and constantly print up all those lists in *Variety* and *The Hollywood Reporter* of the Most Powerful This and That in Hollywood: women, minorities, directors, agents. That way, everyone who's on the list can go to sleep at night feeling one hundred percent powerful and totally in control of their lives; whereas if you are a moderately successful TV writer with a brain tumor pressing on your frontal lobe, a fibroid on your left ovary, and some other, newly discovered gynecological abnormality that's probably going to kill you—then you're probably not sleeping much anyway.

∾

Maybe *that's* why I've been feeling so sad lately? Why I'm constantly on the verge of tears even when tears don't really seem warranted—like when we're forced to celebrate something in the writers' room, or when I'm stuck in traffic on Barham and the voice of the hugely successful TV writer whose phone I used to answer reaches out to me through space and time.

Not in any sort of weird magical-realist, García Márquez–type way.

No, just because he's the guest tonight on *Fresh Air* with Terry Gross.

Or, here's another example of some sadness that should definitely make the Top Five: last night, when pizza arrived on the set for the second meal, I walked a sad, despairing walk across the lot, back to the office, to make myself a peanut butter and banana sandwich; and even though I walk that same stretch of lot virtually every day with Jill on our fake-that-we're-going-to-get-coffee afternoon walk, this time it was cold and dark and I was alone. And when I tried to call my friend Danny in New York to tell him about my impending death from a strange gynecological issue, he didn't pick up, so I guess that made me feel even more alone. Except, of course, for all those mangy stray cats you always see whenever you have to walk across the lot at night. Someone is obviously feeding those cats. I don't know who or why, but when I got back to the office, Dave was there—he also happened to be working late—and we ended up talking for a while in the kitchen about the cats and who feeds them and where everybody else was and lots of other stuff that didn't really mean anything, but it made me feel better in that moment to talk to someone.

Anyone.

Or maybe specifically to Dave.

That's the thing about Dave. Everything he does and says and even wears remind me so vividly of all the people I knew in my youth, that last night as we were talking, some odd sense memory kicked in, and for a second, I was twenty-four again and standing in the kitchen of my Brooklyn apartment. It wasn't a Proustian thing—you know, one of those memories based on tasting or smelling some food you used to love—because even though I was making myself a peanut butter and banana sandwich, I swear I never used to eat peanut butter and banana sandwiches back when I was young and lived in Brooklyn.

Plus, I can't really smell or taste anything right now because I have a cold.

And a small brain tumor pressing on my olfactory nerve.

No, I think my brain made this connection because it was late and no one else was around, and the last time I was alone in a kitchen with a boy talking about alternative rock with any degree of earnestness, I actually *was* twenty-four. And I guess some part of me must miss all those people I knew back then, or the person I was, or something about those times, those long-distant days *before* I moved to LA and became such a moderate success in the entertainment industry.

Only I don't know what it is I could possibly miss.

Truly, I don't.

At the time, those days really didn't seem so great to me. Like back in my early twenties, when I worked at the alternative newspaper, I would always wind up crying in the stairwell every Tuesday night because I just couldn't face any additional proofreader queries, or another Critic's Choice that needed to be edited, or I couldn't convince the Communist film critic to change something the managing editor wanted him to change. When I look back on those times, it doesn't seem to me that I was so outrageously happy. At least now if my job makes me want to cry, I have my own office to do it in, and that seems like a definite improvement. But I guess I must have had something back then that I don't have anymore, right? Something I lost along the way? I swear I don't know what it is, but there must be something I had then that I don't have now. Something I'm missing? Otherwise, I wouldn't get so nostalgic whenever Dave starts going on about some band he loves. It always seems unbelievably poignant to me when he does that. Like last night when I asked him what he was doing this weekend, he said he was driving to San Diego to see Stephen Malkmus, and when I asked him why he didn't just see Stephen Malkmus last week at the El Rey, he said he couldn't because that exact same night he had to see My Morning Jacket at the Wiltern. When I was young, I used to have conversations like that *all the time*. Back then, I could barely get through a day without some guy in vintage clothes going on and on to me about Stephen Malkmus or concert venues or who was playing where on what night. Only I never seem to have conversations like that anymore.

I just don't.

Somewhere along the way to thirty-eight, I stopped having them. I guess that makes sense, since by this age everyone has jobs and/or children they're inordinately obsessed with, so no one really gives a shit anymore about which band is playing where, and even the people who don't have jobs and/or children they're inordinately obsessed with don't really give a shit because—well, to be frank, most people who work in the entertainment industry don't have any idea who Stephen Malkmus is, so there's no way they're driving to San Diego to see him.

Of course, the other big topic Dave is always going on about is that elusive girlfriend of his and how much he wants to break up with her.

And that's less poignant to me.

Obviously, I don't know her. In all this time, I've never met Dave's girlfriend, but whenever he goes on about her, I always tend to go into Teenage Melodrama

Work Mode and break the situation down into scenes and think about it from the point of view of all the different characters involved, and then I assign each character an intention and a goal, and whoever she is, Dave's elusive girlfriend clearly deserves to have a boyfriend who's head over heels in love with her.

That's her goal, right?

Her motivation.

Her intention.

Again, I don't know her, but I doubt she ever sat around as a girl wishing and hoping that one day she'd have a totally Wishy-Washy boyfriend who stays late at the office talking to other girls about how much he wants to break up with her. She probably wanted to have someone who loved her and thought she was special. That's it, right? That's the ultimate motivation everyone seems to be working with in GirlWorld: the shoe girls, the actress-girls, the girls who bring me coffee. They all seem to have this weirdly touching faith that their lives will be made perfect by love, which is a strange philosophy that somehow just never occurred to me when I was younger. Now that I think about it, I guess this begs the question of Dave's goal, his motivation, the thing he's striving so hard to get. But that seems pretty clear to me. I mean, duh...

He wants to break up with his girlfriend.

In fact, the other day it occurred to me that perhaps the *reason* Dave spends so much time talking to me about how much he wants to break up with his girlfriend is that on some deeply subconscious level he wants my *help* in breaking up with his girlfriend. Could that be right? Certainly, if I deleted myself from this story and recast the female lead with a ridiculously beautiful actress-girl, or a shoe girl, or pretty much *any* girl who's not a thirty-eight-year-old, size-fourteen, brain-tumor-ridden spinster, distracted and depressed because of her impending death from a gynecological issue, it's likely that some second-act complications might ensue. The new female lead would probably be all sympathetic and vulnerable and take Dave's side a lot more frequently than I do. She'd touch his arm, maybe toss her chemically straightened hair. And then during February sweeps, the two main characters in this saga would end up having sex, causing the shitty situation with Dave's girlfriend to get much shittier, but at least it would come to a head in some way instead of dragging on for years and years and nearly killing the girl as it did in the case of the not-so-young Miss Frances Burney and that asshole clergyman.

But I don't really know any of this for sure.

It's just a theory I have.

After all, if someone talks to you at great length about a problem they're having, usually they want your help with it, right? I'm not exactly sure because I don't talk to other people at great length about my problems. It's considered vaguely ridiculous to bore people with stories of your personal difficulties when you're a spinster (cf. Miss Bates in *Emma*). Also, it's always been my experience that other people make matters *worse* in a crisis, like tomatoes you have to pick around in a salad. Although I guess I did tell Jill about my latest gynecological ailment and that helped. Maybe we all need that? Someone to talk to so we don't go mad? That was Fanny's big problem when she took that shitty job working for the Queen, especially after the King actually did go mad and Colonel Digby jilted her for Miss Gunning and her 10,000 pounds. That was a rough year for Fanny—the year she turned thirty-eight, arguably the worst of her life. And it's not even like Colonel Digby actually needed that 10,000 pounds. You know, like in *Pride and Prejudice*, when Mr. Wickham is rumored to be courting a Miss King who has 10,000 pounds, or in *Sense and Sensibility*, when Willoughby jilts Marianne for Miss Grey and her 50,000 pounds. Digby *wasn't* some hot young Regency rake with good manners, bad morals, and an even worse credit rating. No, the guy was a forty-six-year-old, depressive, gouty widower with four children and some of his front teeth missing, but for some reason Fanny took a liking to him, and he obviously took a liking to Fanny, because in November 1788 when the King started going mad and the entire court was cut off from civilization and confined to the palace at Kew for one of the coldest, most depressing winters on record—way more depressing than the one we're having now—he started hanging out all the time in Fanny's room.

That's right.

Hanging out.

If I've schooled you well, you should know that this is going to end badly.

~

Oh, sure, for a while things seemed promising. I can't tell you how often during this sad, mad part of the diaries, Fanny returns to her room at the end of some shitty, depressing day to find Colonel Digby just sitting there waiting to talk to her.

And that seems kind of sweet, right?

It won't happen till Part Five of my six-part miniseries—if I ever get there—and obviously it's going to be difficult to convey to modern audiences just how shameful and dangerous it was, circa 1790, for a gouty widower and a lady novelist to be hanging out *completely alone* in the lady's bedroom. It caused a fair amount of scandal at the time, but in the end, Fanny decided that she didn't care about the scandal because it was so nice to have someone to talk to while the King was going mad. Actually, now that I think about it…that's basically what happened last night when I came back from the set and Dave was there. Not that anyone's gone mad on the set. Nope, things haven't gotten *that* bad.

At least not yet.

No, last night Dave and I just stood there in the kitchen and talked, which is exactly the kind of thing Fanny and Digby would have done while the King was going mad—except that we talked about *30 Rock*, and they talked about Pope's *Essay on Man* and other eighteenth-century hot topics, like whether earthly happiness is possible. Another difference is that I never form any expectations that Dave might possibly marry me and take me away from my shitty, depressing job waiting on the Queen.

Not that Fanny actually had those expectations.

She always claimed in the pages of her diary that her heart was safe, that she didn't *love* the Honorable Stephen Digby. Still, she must have thought about what she would do if he proposed. How it would change her life. When you're twenty-two and Thomas Barlow doesn't *hit your fancy*, you turn him down. But when you're thirty-eight and you've spent the preceding three and half years trapped in a castle with a mad King, a passive-aggressive Queen, and a tyrannical German boss, you probably give the matter some serious thought. You probably think to yourself...

                    FANNY (V.O.)
          Sure, I could marry that gouty,
          depressive widower with the
          four kids and the missing front

`teeth. No biggie. No big whoop.`

Basically, he was all she had at that point.

His friendship.

His conversation.

His concern for her well-being.

It's important to keep that in mind.

Sure, back in the real world—outside the palace walls—Fanny had tons of friends and family members who cared about her, but once they all rallied together and convinced her to take the glamorous, super high-paying job working for the Queen? Well, basically then she never got to see any of those people again. She was super busy, of course—that always cuts into your social life. But working at court isn't like a regular job. You can't just leave at the end of the night and drive home in your Volkswagen Beetle convertible. No, once you accept the job, you're basically stuck.

For life.

Without parole.

Fanny knew that going in, but she didn't know she'd have to answer to a bell and get up at six every morning and spend years of her life—years, mind you—playing piquet with her horrible boss, Mrs. Schwellenberg. Also, when she took the job, she had no idea the King would go mad. No one could have predicted that turn of events, or that Digby would jilt her for Miss Gunning and her 10,000 pounds. Oh, wait—shit.

Sorry.

That last one's not true.

Basically, any reasonable person hanging around the court of King George III in the late 1780s could have predicted that the Queen's Vice Chamberlain, the Honorable Stephen Digby, was eventually going to marry Miss Gunning and her 10,000 pounds. As early as February 1788, rumors were flying all over court about it. The courtiers knew. The servants knew. Even the mad King knew: he raved about it in one of his deliriums.

True, *Fanny* didn't see it coming.

But I guess sometimes when you're extremely close to a situation, you just don't see things that other people see. Like when I'm Journaling for Anxiety™, I'm probably missing out on a lot of crucial stuff that's happening around me, like stuff about Dave or the shoe girls or why the set is constantly on the brink of mutiny. That's why I get so annoyed with Fanny's biographers (especially the super bitchy and judgmental one who shall remain nameless). Sure, Fanny should have seen it coming—the jilting, the heartbreak. After all, the exact same thing had happened to her before, had it not? You know, with that evil bastard of a clergyman. Yet, *still*, she didn't see it coming. For some strange reason, you can't see these things coming when they're coming directly at you.

You just can't.

You can only see them when they're about to smash

into other people. Like back when I was a struggling, twentysomething assistant-girl, I remember my boss—the same one I just heard on the radio—making this random comment about how maybe I was taking my whole "spinster" thing too far. At the time, I really didn't get what he meant by that. I think I was probably sitting at my desk reading *The House of Mirth* when he said it to me, and since he went to an even more famous Ivy League school than I did, he probably knew that *The House of Mirth* didn't end well for the main spinster involved. Or I guess it's also possible that I was sitting at my desk reading some book about the eighteenth century because—drum roll, please—back when I was a struggling, twentysomething assistant-girl, I was already somewhat obsessed with Frances Burney, Mother of English Fiction.

Yes, it's true.

I wasn't *crazy* obsessed. I had not yet begun working on my ill-fated, six-part miniseries, but I would often spend my Saturdays downtown at the Central Library checking out books about Fanny or Mrs. Thrale or Dr. Johnson or even Boswell's *London Journal* (even though Fanny and Boswell only crossed paths in a tangential way) and then, because I couldn't afford to actually *buy* these books, I would bring them in to work with me and Xerox all the pertinent parts for free.

You know, in between other late-twentieth-century-style tasks like answering the phone and keeping the minifridge stocked with Mango Snapple.

And whenever I would get bummed about my place in the universe or feel put-upon or start to fear that I would never actually get ahead in the entertainment industry, I would think about Fanny and all the horrible shit she had to endure when she was working for the Queen.

How from 6 a.m. to midnight every day, her time was never her own.

How she had to walk backward in the presence of royalty.

How she wasn't allowed to wear her spectacles in company.

Plus, Fanny was already thirty-four years old when she got that job *and* the most successful female novelist alive on the planet; I was only twenty-seven when I was a struggling, put-upon Hollywood assistant, and obviously my duties weren't *so* oppressive because they left me tons of free time to work on my *NewsRadio* spec script, read Boswell's *London Journal*, and make conversation with all the people who were constantly hanging around my desk waiting to talk to my boss. To be honest, I don't really remember much of what we would talk about day in and day out—although I suspect that some of them got treated to stories about Frances Burney and her career difficulties or stories from Boswell's *London Journal*—even though, like I said, Fanny and Boswell didn't really interact that much. They knew each other, but they weren't, like, super close, and when he came to see her at Windsor Palace circa 1790 to ask if he could use some of her personal letters from Dr. Johnson in an innovative new biography he was writing, she totally blew him off—which I know makes her sound like a pill, but obviously the book did okay even without her help; if not in sales, then at least in world historical terms.

Of course, nowadays things aren't like that.

Nowadays, whenever I'm stuck in an office conversation, it's generally about the romantic difficulties of some girl in her early thirties—her attempts to find "The One" and so on and so forth—and that leaves very little time to talk about Fanny or Boswell. This is a definite sign of progress: it shows that lady writers are finally muscling their way into the industry! Back when I first started out, there were hardly any of them, and as I believe I've mentioned before, *guys* who work on TV shows don't generally spend sixteen hours a day talking about their romantic difficulties.

Especially not guys who work on *animated* TV shows.

Some of them barely talk at all. They tend to be really shy, and I hate to generalize, but the ones who *aren't* really shy, are mostly just focusing really hard on getting ahead in the entertainment industry, and that's fine. I've got no beef with people trying to get ahead in the entertainment industry (after all, they are my people), but back then, this impulse of theirs was a giant pain in my ass, because in their mad rush to get ahead in the entertainment industry, they were constantly hanging out at my desk reading my boss's trades, and if I didn't watch them like a hawk, they would frequently *steal* his trades, and then I would be in trouble later on when my boss went looking for *Daily Variety* and couldn't find it.

But whatever.

I'm over it.

This story happened ages ago, and all the principals involved have gone on to enjoy at least moderate success in the entertainment industry, so there's really no point in holding a grudge. Obviously, they weren't all bad, all these male TV writers I worked with back then. Some of them were quite nice, actually. There was even this one who gave me a ride home a couple times when my car was in the shop, and he bought me a book.

Or maybe he just *gave* me a book.

You know, like after he had finished it and didn't know what to do with it. I'm not sure about that part, but it meant a lot to me at the time, because back when I was a struggling, put-upon Hollywood assistant, I didn't have tons of disposable income to spend on books. I couldn't just walk into a bookstore and buy any old book I wanted, which is what I do now, and it's obviously what that guy was doing because he was probably like ten years older than me and already a much bigger success in the entertainment industry than I'll ever be. He had great credits, this guy.

Seriously.

He'd worked on some *amazing* television shows, and even though career success and writing ability don't always go together, he also happened to be a really great writer and, now that I think about it, possibly a functioning alcoholic of some sort. That's something the younger writers were always trying to get me to believe about this guy. According to them, he often smelled like alcohol, and even though I never smelled the alcohol myself, I can see how this legend got started. He had this look about him, this vaguely unhealthy look, like a tubercular, nineteenth-century literary genius. He was tall and thin with sort of a sunken air, and he did have a tendency to show up late looking rumpled and dissolute. That never bothered me much, except when he didn't show up at all—then I'd have to make a bunch of phone calls all over town looking for him because back then, people didn't have cell phones so much. I suppose it's entirely possible, looking back in a clear-eyed way at the situation, that the reason I never smelled alcohol on the Tubercular Genius and everybody else did, was that I had a bit of a soft spot for the guy.

You know, that I had some type of crush on him.

But then it's also possible—and Brain Surgeon #1 swears this could be true—that from the time I was born, I already had a small, barely noticeable subfrontal midline meningioma pressing on my olfactory nerve, and this naturally would have made it harder for me to sniff out the functioning show-biz alcoholics in my midst. I do remember the Tubercular Genius sitting across from me at my desk one lazy afternoon and telling me a story that involved him falling asleep by his pool and accidentally sleeping outdoors all night. At the time, I was so impressed that a really great TV writer was talking to me—and, bonus, he had a pool!—that I failed to pick up on how much sleeping outside all night by your pool sounds exactly like the sort of thing an alcoholic would do.

Of course, now that I have lived in LA for more than a decade and met a zillion people who have their own pools, I totally get that nuance. Most of them aren't falling asleep *outside* on any kind of a regular basis.

But circa 1997, the Tubercular Genius was always doing these things that I found adorably absentminded and writerly, like falling asleep by his pool and asking me what his own phone number was, and it never occurred to me back then that these were bad things.

Which again seems to point in the general direction of my having had a soft spot for the Tubercular Genius.

He did, after all, give me a book, one that was set— or at least partially set—in the late eighteenth century, which is either a really huge coincidence or else the Tubercular Genius had put some thought into the matter and noticed a common theme to my reading material. I think it even occurred to me back then that the Tubercular Genius might have given me this book because he was interested in me in some sort of romantic or sexual way. I don't think that nuance had to be explained to me way after the fact, as it usually does with these types of scenarios. Like here's an example of that phenomenon...

Senior year in college, I'm watching TV with my friend Julie when my phone rings. I get up to answer it, and it's this boy who always sits next to me in my comp lit seminar. Since it's 1990 and we're the sort of college students who take comp lit seminars, we talk for a while about *Twin Peaks*, and then he asks me if I want to go to a movie. I tell him I can't because I don't have any money. Later, when I rehash the gist of this conversation to Julie, she informs me in no uncertain terms that Comp Lit Guy was "asking me out." At the time, I refused to accept her analysis of the situation, although in later years I have come to see that her side of the argument might have had some merit.

Of course, I still have no idea what Comp Lit Guy *himself* was actually thinking, and at this point, I think it's safe to say I never will. What's kind of a fucked-up coincidence is that very same Comp Lit Guy randomly moved to LA last December and took me out for Korean food right before I found out about my brain tumor, and even though it was nice to see him again and all that, it's not like he tried to kiss me or even walked me to my car, so in a way I think my original assessment of the situation was probably accurate.

I think he really was just looking for someone to go to a movie with.

With the Tubercular Genius, the possibility that he might have been interested in me was a lot more obvious because the flirting—if that's technically what it was—was centered on books and happened to replicate a very famous incident from the first act of *Hannah and Her Sisters*: the part when Michael Caine "accidentally" runs into Barbara Hershey and buys her some e.e. cummings and tells her to read the poem on page 112, and truly you'd have to be a complete idiot not to understand what that scene's about.

It's about sex.

And actually now that I think about it, so was the book the Tubercular Genius gave me. Not in any kind of obvious way. I mean, it wasn't pornographic or anything, but it was written by Milan Kundera, and isn't everything Milan Kundera writes basically about sex? This particular book—I swear I still have it someplace—was all about the art of seduction and how they went about practicing it in the eighteenth century versus how people go about doing it nowadays, which is obviously *way* up my alley. So again, hats off to the Tubercular Genius for figuring this out about me—and hats off to *me* for actually having the GirlWorld smarts back then to consider the possibility that the Tubercular Genius may have meant something by this gesture. After all, back then I did happen to be in possession of the two main attributes the men of contemporary, twenty-first-century LA always seem to find so alluring in a female companion...

I was still in my twenties, and I made a lot less money than he did.

So, yes, it did occur to me back then that the Tubercular Genius might have been interested in me in some sort of romantic or sexual way. That thought did occur to me at the time, although I guess it didn't occur to me that if I played my cards right, I could end up being *Mrs.* Tubercular Genius, which is what Jill swears the shoe girls are thinking all the time as they're going about their daily lives. And I quote...

                    JILL
        Every time they meet a man,
        the first question they ask
        themselves—the very first thing
        that pops into their minds—is
        "Is this my husband? Is he The
        One? My soulmate? My destiny?"

And that right there is very instructional to me. Because when I meet a man, mostly what I am thinking is...

                    ME (V.O.)
        Please don't let this person
        hand me some sort of spec script
        I'm going to have to read.

See? That's interesting, right? Quite revelatory. In fact, now that I think about it, there was this one morning when the Tubercular Genius showed up way early at the office, which meant we were alone, and I remember there being this strange tension in the air, but it's not like the Tubercular Genius leapt across the room and kissed me like Michael Caine ultimately winds up doing in *Hannah and Her Sisters*, thus moving the plot forward in an incredibly elegant, efficient manner that's also really funny when the record gets scratched and Daniel Stern and Max von Sydow walk back into the room arguing about puce.

No, I'm pretty sure what actually happened was that the phone rang, and since it was my job back then to answer the phone, I'm one hundred percent certain that I answered it. I didn't just let it ring and go to voicemail, which is probably what the girl in this story would have done if she had been super focused on becoming Mrs. Tubercular Genius. Whereas a girl who is super focused on getting ahead in the entertainment industry—well, that girl is probably going to pick up the goddamn phone because if it's ringing at that hour it's probably her boss, so that's why it's not a very good story, the one about me and the Tubercular Genius.

Shoot.

Now I'm sorry I wasted all that time Journaling for Anxiety™ about it. It's a real non-starter of a story, isn't it? Way worse than the one about Fanny and her too-handsome cousin, the portrait painter. Basically, the whole thing just ends in some weird, anticlimactic misunderstanding. Obviously, I should have stuck with the story of Fanny getting jilted by the not-so-Honorable Stephen Digby, i.e., Part Five of my six-part miniseries. That at least had some stakes to it, some potential to be entertaining and, heck, I could go on forever and ever about all that heartbreaking stuff. About how Digby didn't even have the guts to tell Fanny in person that he was jilting her for Miss Gunning. Nope. Instead, she had to hear it from her spinster colleague Miss Planta, and even then she didn't actually *believe* it until two days later, when Miss Planta informed her that the Princesses had publicly wished Miss Gunning joy in the drawing room.

Or, I could go on and on about the good times.

About the time Digby made her laugh by asking her how much ribbon she had in her bonnet. Or the time he picked up Pope's *Essay on Man* and read charming passages till the clock struck ten. Or the time he looked at her and suddenly exclaimed out of nowhere...

DIGBY

How amazingly well you have
borne all this!

I could keep Journaling for Anxiety™ about all that stuff and more, but the good news is that I won't. I'm tired. I've had a rough day...

Week.

Month.

Year.

But there's really no point in going on and on about this stuff anymore. No point in trying to research and untangle a bunch of eighteenth-century creative struggles, lurking fevers, financial woes, and romantic difficulties. You see, when I got back from my holiday travels on December 30, I had a letter waiting for me from the BBC. Turns out they have rejected my proposal for a lavishly produced, six-part miniseries about Frances Burney, Mother of English Fiction. They get a lot of submissions etc., etc., &c., and they just didn't feel like mine had any merit. So I guess the good news is I don't have to wonder about what I would do if they had accepted my proposal and made all my dreams come true. Now I can just move on and—what? Giving up doesn't seem like an option. It did hurt when I got home from my holiday travels and found that letter waiting for me. It wasn't a very pleasant way to end the year—you know, having all my hopes and dreams *officially* dashed—but since the year started with finding out I had a brain tumor, it wasn't shaping up to be one of the absolute best of my life anyway. Plus, the script for Episode 16 was due in three days, and I signed the contract and so on and so forth, so basically I had no choice. I just had to keep writing. That's what Fanny would have done.

In fact, it's what she did do.

No matter how bleak and hopeless things got—no matter how low she fell—she just kept writing.

FRIDAY, FEBRUARY 23, 2007

IT'S OFFICIAL. Indecision over. Second-act problem solved.

I'm going to have brain surgery.

I'm going to be brave, suck it up, and do it. I may as well, right? I mean it's just a little brain surgery.

It's not like being trapped in a castle with a mad King, a passive-aggressive Queen, and a tyrannical German boss.

Or getting jilted by Colonel Digby.

It's nothing compared to what the spinsters of the past had to endure. Governessing. Living with their mothers. Falling prey to adventurers, if they were rich. *Not* falling prey to adventurers, if they weren't rich. Heck, what I've got isn't even a life-threatening illness, like *ovarian cancer*, which is the life-threatening illness I totally thought I had for a while there back in January, when I seemed to be losing my shit and crying all the time in the workplace.

January, it turns out, was my Devastating Setback/Point of No Return (Rule #20), i.e., the moment when all hope seems lost.

In retrospect, I should have known that because of the tears—romantic comedy heroines *always* tend to sob uncontrollably near the end of the movie, usually when they're all dressed up for some big event. For me, it came not at my best friend's wedding, a super high-stakes client dinner, or an awards ceremony, but last Friday afternoon at 1:45 p.m. at the radiology place on Wilshire and LaPeer. After all that watching and waiting and scanning and probing—after thirteen months of it—that's when I finally just lost it and started sobbing uncontrollably in one of their tiny little changing rooms. When the technician lady came to get me, I tried to explain to her, mid-sob, exactly why I was sobbing, but she didn't seem too fazed by me and all my third-act craziness.

She was actually the same technician who'd given me two previous ultrasounds, the one in June and the one in January, which was kind of nice, to see a familiar face in that context. Before starting the horrifically painful test, she decided to do another ultrasound—cool, whatever, I'm used to that. But after she did it, she left the room for a very long time (obviously you would edit this part out in the movie version), and I just kept crying and crying, and when she came back, she had this radiologist with her—a silver-haired gentleman in a white lab coat who looked like he should be *playing* a radiologist in a Woody Allen movie—and he appeared quite visibly annoyed with the crying. You could tell he was totally over it, like, hello, no one wants to see the thirty-eight-year-old wacky best-friend character break down crying, even if it is her Point of No Return. But there really wasn't much I could do about the crying, and in my defense, I did *stop* crying when he told me the good news...

SILVER-HAIRED RADIOLOGIST
Well, you're just fine. There's
absolutely nothing here at all.

Or words to that effect.

That's not an *exact* quote. I mean it is an exact quote from *Hannah and Her Sisters*, but it's not what the silver-haired radiologist actually said to me that day, because it was a while ago now and it's not like I took out a pen and jotted it all down. Basically, he just told me that I was free to go because—voilà, whatever weird thing was abnormal on my last ultrasound wasn't abnormal anymore. So I just got dressed and went back to the set of Episode 16 for the rest of the day, and I have to say...

I don't think I've ever been so happy to be on the set.

I didn't even care that we shot until 2 a.m. that Fraturday night, and if I really did experience a Climactic Moment of Character Growth (Rule # 25) following my Point of No Return, I suppose for the rest of my life I will always enjoy the set. I can see now how it's not the worst place in the world, especially compared to the radiology place at Wilshire and LaPeer. It's especially fun if you hang out with the sound guy who always has Altoids or ask the DP for stories about when he used to work on *Magnum P.I.* Sometimes you have to talk to the actors, but what's more important, when you're a writer-producer on a set, is to *listen* to the actors. Because no matter what age or gender they are, most actors are a lot like teenage girls: they're inordinately obsessed with their hair, and what they want more than anything else in the world is reassurance from some type of authority figure—someone who seems like she knows what she's doing. The missing piece of the puzzle I never had before is that I *am* an authority figure.

I am a person who seems like she knows what she's doing.

Someone who's brave and tough and bold and confident.

Someone who's totally going to have brain surgery. I just pulled the trigger and called the brain surgeon's office a few minutes ago, and they're going to get back to me right away with a date. Turns out you only have to give them like two weeks' notice if you want to have brain surgery. It's not like getting your hair dyed or your eyebrows tweezed, which has to be scheduled *months* in advance. My little sister promised to fly in from the Midwest, but until we know the exact date, we can't get her a plane ticket, so now the only thing left to do is wait. And frankly, I'm used to that. I could watch a little TV, except that over the weekend something went horribly wrong with my TiVo and now I can't figure out how to hook it all back up, so basically it's like a huge part of me—everything I ever recorded on that TiVo—

is irrevocably lost and can never be recovered.

An episode of *Taxi* from 1978 about Angela the fat girl.

A Bette Davis movie from Turner Classic Movies that isn't available on DVD.

Three episodes of a superhero show Arnie Greenblatt wants me to watch because he thinks he can maybe get me a job there when the show I'm on now inevitably gets canceled.

In an instant, it was all lost, and I've got absolutely no way to get it back. Except for Dave, I guess.

That's sort of vaguely hopeful, isn't it?

Dave did offer to come over some time and fix my TiVo for me, which was totally nice of him, although I'm sure he won't actually do it because no one in LA ever really does anything they say they're going to do. It's just not the LA way. For a long time, I thought I was imagining this phenomenon, but apparently they actually discuss it in the *Lonely Planet Guide to Southern California*. Comp Lit Guy told me this last year when he took me out for Korean food that resembled weeds. He'd lived all over the world in the fifteen years since college—Siberia, Nepal, Mongolia, the Sichuan province, all over South America—and for a while he was a diplomat in Switzerland; yet before he moved to LA, he still felt compelled to consult the *Lonely Planet Guide to Southern California* in order to get to a grip on the strange ways and alien customs we have here.

He didn't last long in LA. After a couple months, he moved back to New York, and I can't say I blame him. I know everyone jokes about it all the time, especially in Woody Allen movies, but I'm starting to think maybe there is something truly awful about LA. Maybe there's something in the water here? Obviously, it would have to be in the bottled water. Something that makes people lie all the time and constantly say they're going to do things that they don't really do.

Although I swear I really am going to have brain surgery.

Obviously, yes, there's a great opportunity here for me to get in one last round of second-guessing. After all, hospitals are terrifyingly germ-filled places, surgeons routinely amputate the wrong limbs, etc., etc., &c. But fuck it, now that I'm past the Point of No Return, it's far too late to think about all that shit.

Really.

Seriously.

I had to put a thousand-dollar deposit on my Visa card, and I'm pretty sure they won't give it back if I chicken out.

ON MY LAST DAY at the office, the winner of the shoe contest offered me a solution to my spinster problem. She didn't call it that, but we both knew what she meant. She says that if I go to a place called Café Stella in Silver Lake, sit with a book, and have a drink, a guy will come up and talk to me. That's it. That's the plan for how I would cross over to the other side and become a full-time, non-spinster resident of GirlWorld—the kind of girl who has Love Interests and goes on dates. It's simple. It's elegant. And I'm sure it would work except for one thing: I'm me, and I don't look even the slightest bit like the shoe girl who suggested this plan. I am not six feet tall and blond and really skinny, so no matter how long I sit reading a book in a fashionable Silver Lake café, a guy is never actually going to come up and talk to me.

But I appreciated the advice.

It was clearly offered from a place of friendship and goodwill. The whole reason we started discussing the subject in the first place was that she said she liked my dress. It's black and sort of '50s inspired, and of course I found it on the sale rack at guess where? Banana Republic. So it's not really all that exciting. Mostly I just bought it because it looked like the sort of thing a grieving widow might wear in an Italian neo-realist movie. She said it looked great on me, though, and that's when she laid out the plan for how I would leave behind The Spinster Way and cross over to the other side. She said that after work, while I was still wearing the dress, I should go to a bar, and then perhaps sensing that she had already lost me, she named a specific bar—Café Stella in Silver Lake—and said I should go there and sit at the bar and have a glass of wine and read a book: an interesting, vaguely European book. I believe Camus was suggested, and I think she also may have advised me to keep my sunglasses on indoors, but she definitely closed with a promise that if I did all these things, a guy would come up and talk to me. I remember that part because it seemed so completely at odds with all my previous life experience, but I'm sure it's exactly the sort of thing that happens to her all the time as she goes about her LA existence. Otherwise she wouldn't have said it with such conviction.

Oh, and she also suggested I have an affair with my brain surgeon.

Apparently, that happened to one of her friends who had to have surgery for something. I don't know her at all (the friend of the shoe girl, that is), but I'm sure she was a shoe girl as well. You'd kind of have to be, wouldn't you? To end up sleeping with the guy who's cutting you open. Me, I could have ten consecutive brain tumors—they could cut this one out of me tomorrow morning at 8:15 a.m. and nine others could grow back in its place—and *still*, it would never occur to me that I should try to sleep with the brain surgeon.

Just like it's never occurred to me to try and set the brain surgeon up with any of my single friends.

I got in trouble for that the other night. I was having dinner with some female writer-friends who knew I was about to have brain surgery, and one of them asked me a very LA question. She asked me what the brain surgeon looked like. I had never given the matter much thought, but one of the brain surgeon's distinguishing physical characteristics is that he's black—you know, of African American descent—and apparently, it's a pretty big crime in GirlWorld if you meet an African American brain surgeon and fail to pry into his personal life and attempt to set him up with all of your single, African American female friends. At the very least you're supposed to do some sort of due diligence. You've got to get in there and *investigate* the successful African American professional you've met and make sure he's not the same one your friend is *supposed* to marry. Otherwise, she might have to be single forever and then it would be all your fault. I don't know—maybe it was just the fourteen-dollar raspberry lemon drop I was drinking—but I have to say that kinda blew my mind.

All the progress I thought I had made in understanding the shoe girls and the bizarre, unfathomable ways of GirlWorld suddenly went right out the window.

Basically, what she was saying was that in Girl-World, not only are you supposed to be constantly on the lookout for your own husband—you know, like Jill says the shoe girls are—but I guess you're also supposed to be watching out all the time for *other girls' husbands*. Frankly, I don't know how everyone in GirlWorld is able to accomplish this and still have time left over to shop for $500 shoes. To me, it all just sounds incredibly exhausting.

Much worse than having brain surgery.

Although not as bad as having to face your brain surgeon after one of your Hollywood screenwriter friends has called his office and inquired about his marital status.

That's kind of embarrassing, don't you think? I'll have to mention it to him at some point, won't I? Like should I apologize for it? Or can I just ignore it? What's the etiquette here? I swear I could tell you exactly how all the various members of the Bennet family are supposed to act at the Netherfield ball—how Mary shouldn't play the piano so long and Kitty and Lydia shouldn't chase the officers and Mrs. Bennet shouldn't talk so loudly about what an uptight douchebag Mr. Darcy is—but I have no idea what you're supposed to do when one of your Hollywood screenwriter friends calls your brain surgeon and tries to set him up with another one of your Hollywood screenwriter friends. I'm just not prepared to deal with that eventuality right now.

Why do we all have to go to all this trouble anyway? Why do we have to be calling people up we don't even know and asking them about their marital status and working every minute of our lives to get skinnier and prettier and driving across the country in diapers like that crazy astronaut lady who tried to kill someone or something? That caused a little mini-debate in the room the other day. Jill was pro–crazy astronaut lady. She thought it sounded pretty cool—you know, the way love could be so strong and powerful that it would make you do crazy things like that. Honestly, I don't see the attraction. I mean can't we all just be ourselves and not wear makeup and die alone? That's always seemed like a viable option to me, and I don't understand why more people don't get on board with it. Once you sign all the relevant documents telling them to unplug you if something goes horribly wrong during your brain surgery, it's really not so bad. I mean when you think about it, dying alone is just the way of the world. Or, at least, of the heterosexual world, because women almost always outlive men. That's a known scientific fact. So even the girls who've won the ultimate grand prize in all of GirlWorld, the prize that's bigger than sleeping with actors or winning the shoe contest or getting your pilot picked up—even the ones who have actually gone out there and somehow managed to find this elusive quantity known as True Love—well, most of them are going to die alone, too.

After all, that is what happened to Fanny.

Fanny died alone in Bath on January 6, 1840, at the

ripe old age of eighty-seven.

I think I've mentioned that before. I must be pre-occupied with death or something. Of course, when I say she died alone, I don't mean *totally* alone because of course she had those devoted nieces by her side. I've got three at the moment. Three nieces. But the oldest one is only eight years old, so if I die in a few hours while I'm having brain surgery, it's not super likely that she'll take it upon herself to edit and publish all my Journaling for Anxiety™ the way Fanny's niece Charlotte Barrett did with hers. My two sisters are the ones who would come and clean out my apartment if I died, but since they don't work in the entertainment industry, it's not like they're going to have any idea what to do with the first two parts of an ill-fated, six-part miniseries set in the eighteenth century and two-hundred-some-odd pages of mad ramblings about brain tumors and shoe contests. Even if they did have the wherewithal to give it to my agent, Arnie Greenblatt, he would probably just give them the same speech he's been giving me for the past ten years. You know, the one about how no one's ever going to give a shit about your passion project until you make shitloads of money doing something totally unrelated to your passion project.

Only this time, the speech would be largely wasted on me because I would be dead.

Just like Fanny.

She outlived most of her contemporaries.

All three of her sisters.

Both brothers.

Her friends.

Her coworkers.

Her bosses.

All of her many Love Interests.

That's what happens when you live to be eighty-seven.

Everyone who ever guest-starred in your diaries goes before you.

The Honorable Stephen Digby died the same year as Fanny's favorite sister, Susanna. He didn't even make it into the nineteenth century. And you know what's kind of sad and weird? Miss Gunning, with her 10,000 pounds, the one who bested Fanny and got the honor of becoming *Mrs.* Honorable Stephen Digby? She lived only four more years after she won that honor.

Boswell died in 1795, but based on what I've read of his diaries, Boswell had a lot of venereal diseases, so I'm kinda surprised he lasted that long.

Edmund Burke, who has the distinction of being the only person in Fanny's diaries more nearsighted than Fanny—he died in 1797.

Jeremiah Crutchley, who loved to hunt and thought Johnson's *Life of Pope* was the best of his Lives, died in 1805, at sixty.

Fanny's hip, cool, suspiciously young-looking musician father made it to the advanced age of eighty-eight, and her erstwhile BFF Mrs. Thrale, all the way to eighty. Mad King George III also hit the four-score mark, but his passive-aggressive Queen checked out in her early seventies. So perhaps it's not really so good for you, keeping all your aggression on the inside. Oh, shit, I really am doing it, aren't I?

Obsessing about death.

Signing your will *will* do that to you.

Plus, signing tons of other papers deciding what to do with all your money and organs in the event of your untimely death.

Harold, my business manager, set all that up for me, and all I had to do was drive to Beverly Hills and sign. My little sister came with. She's a lot more dependable than the little sister in *Hannah and Her Sisters*. I picked her up at the airport around three, and after we signed all the papers, I was planning to take her by my office and introduce her to everyone—Jill and Dave and whichever shoe girls and delightful twentysomething assistants happened to be around. I was also going to show her the sets and, possibly, god help me, try and introduce her to some of the actors. My little sister's a pretty big fan of the show I've been working on, so I thought she might enjoy that. Plus, if I died, then she'd be able to tell everybody back home in the Rust Belt what a big success I was. How even though I never did manage to lose those last twenty pounds or tell good third-date stories, at least I had made some of my

TV-writing dreams come true and had my own parking space and a chair with my name on it. But signing all those documents related to my own death kinda took it out of me. I didn't think I could handle that *plus* the stress of driving over the hill during rush hour, so I sent Dave an email asking him to tell everybody that I was bailing. Then I took my little sister to my favorite sushi place and called it a night. She's sleeping now in my guest room/office. At least I presume she's sleeping, because it's like 2 a.m.

I am not sleeping.

But then it's probably not hugely important to get a good night's sleep before you have brain surgery. I think it's probably fine to stay up all night thinking about Fanny and how she died on January 6, 1840, with her devoted niece/editor by her side.

Actually, you know what's kind of freaky and always makes me sad?

January 6 was the exact same day her favorite sister, Susanna, died.

That's kind of weird, right? Fanny didn't see her after the fall of 1796, when Molesworth Phillips, Susanna's evil scofflaw of a husband, carted their whole family off to Ireland. Susanna didn't want to go to Ireland—from the get-go, the whole thing sounded like a gigantic drag to her—but her husband had basically kidnapped her eldest son and put him in school there, so what choice did she have? Women didn't have a lot of choices back then. They weren't "empowered" like we are today, with our high heels and constant waxing. So Susanna went to Ireland with her half-mad, unfeeling reprobate of a husband, and while she was in Ireland, she kept getting sicker and sicker, and eventually she did try to come home to England—to see her family and to live, or perhaps to die, among people who actually loved her—but right after she crossed the Irish Sea and landed at a place called Parkgate, she died.

In lodgings.

Which always sounds worse to me than any other kind of dying.

I'm not sure why.

Maybe because it implies that the person who died didn't belong anywhere.

That she was adrift and alone, which Fanny's favorite sister wasn't.

She wasn't alone.

Her brother Charles was with her *and* her half-mad, unfeeling reprobate of a husband, and so was her daughter, Fanny, who was named after—well, it should be pretty obvious who she was named after. It was 1800 by the time Susanna died, the dawn of a new century, and for the next forty years of that century—for the rest of her life—Fanny always observed January 6 as a day of remembrance. You know, like Jewish people have Yom Kippur. Or maybe that's not what Yom Kippur is for—I don't know these things because I had the misfortune to be born Catholic and Italian American. Basically, whatever else she happened to be doing that day, on January 6, Fanny would always stop and take a moment to think about her favorite sister, the one who loved to play the piano and spoke French really well. I'm not exactly sure what she would think about. Forty years is a long time to outlive your favorite sister, so I'm sure it changed from year to year.

In the beginning, Topic A was probably how Susanna never should have married that asshole Molesworth Phillips.

In later years, Fanny probably thought more about the good stuff. You know, about the time they dressed their brother Charles up in a funny outfit and sent him off to the printer with the manuscript of Fanny's first novel. When they did that, they weren't thinking about how much that one simple act might change Fanny's life. They sent it off, she later said, "for a frolic." They weren't thinking that Fanny would become the toast of London, live in fancy houses with Mrs. Thrale, hobnob with Dr. Johnson, and flirt unsuccessfully with Jeremiah Crutchley.

They weren't thinking about how George Owen Cambridge would break Fanny's heart.

And that Stephen Digby would break it again—in the same way.

Or about how god-awful it would be working for the Queen.

So god-awful that in December 1790, Fanny finally worked up the courage to submit her letter of resignation.

That's right.

She *quit* her glamorous, high-paying job.

You know, just like Woody Allen does in *Hannah and Her Sisters*.

And then guess what happened?

Go ahead.

Guess.

It shouldn't be too hard, because it's exactly what happens at the end of every romantic comedy.

She fell in love.

If you are a truly extraordinary person, sometimes it takes a revolution for your love life to improve.

That's what happened in Fanny's case.

There was a revolution.

The French Revolution.

Perhaps you've heard of it? As revolutions go, it's one of the bigger ones. The details aren't important. For the purposes of this story, all you really need to know is that once they started chopping off heads in France, tons of French people ended up living in England, and some of these people—including some interesting French bachelors with deep-set, gray-blue eyes and hair that flowed over their collars—moved in right next door to Fanny's favorite sister, Susanna.

Which I guess is just dumb luck or something.

After all, Fanny didn't *cause* the French Revolution.

She didn't man the barricades or try to hasten it along in any way.

It just happened.

And because it happened—because a bunch of strangers living in France decided that they had had enough of kings and took to the streets and started killing each other—Fanny fell in love.

In the spring of 1793.

When she was forty years old.

With a penniless French émigré named Alexandre d'Arblay. He was thirty-eight, a minor aristocrat, a friend of Lafayette, a general in an army that didn't exist anymore, and here's the thing…

He actually loved her back.

You didn't see that coming, did you?

Neither did Fanny.

Nonetheless, it happened.

Now if I could just figure out *how* it happened—you know, what Fanny did differently this time to make the interesting French bachelor love her back when all the others had not. If I could just unravel that plot twist, I think I could finally give up on my ill-fated, six-part miniseries, stick it in a drawer somewhere, and then you know what I'd write?

A self-help book.

About how to fall in love at the advanced age of forty.

I think a lot of women would want to read that book.

They'd want to know how it's possible for someone to fail so miserably at love for two entire decades and still wind up getting the sort of picture-perfect, story-book happy ending that is normally reserved for pretty, extroverted heroines who look great in sleeveless outfits and devote their whole lives to personal grooming and "putting themselves out there."

There wasn't a makeover montage, if that's what you're thinking.

When they met, Fanny was the same nearsighted, badly dressed novelist she'd always been.

She was still *herself* in every essential way.

Still the same girl who had refused Thomas Barlow, gotten into strange quarrels with Jeremiah Crutchley, and sat next to George Owen Cambridge at parties for too long without telling him to fuck off and leave her alone. She was still the same girl who got jilted for Miss Gunning and her 10,000 pounds. Only way older, of course. And way less successful in the entertainment industry.

Yet Alexandre d'Arblay seems to have been taken with her right from the start.

They met on Tuesday, January 22, 1793—or

possibly, Wednesday the 23rd—and six months later, on Sunday, July 28, 1793, they were married in the church at Mickelham and lived happily ever after.

At least until the British and the French decided to go to war with each other.

And then a bunch of very confusing and hard-to-explain Napoleonic wars happened.

And then in 1818, Alexandre d'Arblay died.

The interesting French bachelor died.

So there's another person Fanny outlived.

Her husband.

Her soulmate.

Her one true love.

On the day he died, he looked up at her with what she described as "sweetness inexpressible" and said...

M. D'ARBLAY
Qui?

Which is French for "who." But according to Fanny, what he actually meant was...

M. D'ARBLAY
Who will be there for you when
you are dying? Who's going to
return the favor and give you
something to drink?

Because I guess at the time she was giving him a beverage of some sort. And when she answered him, she said…

FANNY

You! My dearest Ami! You
yourself! You shall recover, and
take your revenge.

She claims she said it cheerfully, which seems kind of hard to believe given the whole deathbed context, but then maybe if you had to wait until you were forty to meet the man of your dreams, and suddenly there you were at your soulmate's deathbed, and his main topic of conversation was *you* and how things might end up going for *you* after his death—well, then maybe you've done okay for yourself.

Maybe you've managed to get the whole love thing right.

After she said it, he smiled and shut his eyes, and then a few hours later he died. She had to go on for twenty-two more years without him—without the soulmate it had taken her forty years, two novels, tons of lurking fevers, and one really shitty job to find.

Although, perhaps I'm getting ahead of myself.

I seem to have skipped over all the happy parts of the story, the parts where love conquers all. I forget sometimes just how much normal people seem to enjoy those parts. At the very least I should have told you how the interesting French bachelor proposed, but it's not a very good story by contemporary GirlWorld standards because there was no diamond ring involved. All he did was send her a letter. That's it. Just a letter. It's dated "31 March 1793," and in this letter, the interesting French bachelor goes on for pages and pages about some crackpot scheme he has come up with to establish *"un Corps d'artillerie à Cheval qu'on dit que le gouvernement anglais veut lever pour la deffense de ses Côtes."*

Did you catch that?

I think it's something about French cavalry officers. *Cheval* I'm pretty sure is "horse," and *corps d'artillerie* can't be anything other than "artillery corps." Anyway, the impoverished academics who make it their life's work to study Fanny *swear* this letter is a declaration of love—they say it's tantamount to a proposal of marriage—and Fanny seems to have agreed with them because at some point after she received this letter and before she died, she wrote on it *"Precieuses!"*

Like that.

With an exclamation point.

But obviously, this will all have to be changed in the stirring conclusion to my six-part miniseries. Think about it. Even if you had Colin Firth in the part *and* you had him write the letter while he was naked and dripping wet in the bathtub—still, a letter about fencible cavalry would be a big snooze. Admittedly, it does seem romantic the way the interesting French bachelor wrote the letter, got on his horse, and rode all the way to London so he could drop it in the penny post that very same day; but no network currently in existence is going to get on board with that as the stirring conclusion to a six-part miniseries about the fortunes and misfortunes of a little-known, long-dead eighteenth-century novelist who was incredibly nearsighted and had bad fashion sense.

Obviously, a mad dash would have to be made to someplace more exciting than a mailbox.

To a dock, maybe. Docks were basically what they had back then instead of airports. Or, fuck it, maybe there could just be a ball or something? That was always our fallback plan at the teenage melodrama—dress 'em up, slap a song on it, the kids will cry. I'm sure that would work. It wouldn't be true as far as what *actually* happened, but who would know? Just me, I guess. And even *I* don't know what actually happened, because the letter about the fencible cavalry scheme is all in French, and I don't read French. Ironic, isn't it? Here I have spent almost twenty years of my life studying up on Fanny—obsessing on her romantic difficulties, reading all her diaries, her books, her letters, getting to know her family members, her coworkers, getting myself all *invested* in her story—and when we finally get to the Happy Ending (Rule #2), the part that is all about Love, I can't even begin to understand any of it because it's all in French, and I don't speak French.

Or maybe that's not ironic.

Maybe that's totally appropriate, since Love is also

turning out to be a language I don't speak. It just doesn't make sense to my spinster brain the way it does to all the expensively shod residents of GirlWorld, which is either because I was born with a tiny little brain tumor pressing on my frontal lobe in the exact "love" location, or, I suppose, it's also possible that I just never tried hard enough to learn it.

That's basically what happened with French.

I did take it in high school.

I took it for three years.

And then I took it again in college.

So if I concentrate super hard, sometimes I can get the general gist of what's going on with Fanny and her interesting French bachelor.

But only when something incredibly boring is happening.

Like they'll be alone in the parlor, and the interesting French bachelor will be kissing her hand and saying I don't know what, and Fanny will interrupt him with lines like...

                    FANNY
Comment se porte M⁀ᵉ de Staël?

                  M. D'ARBLAY
Très bien.

                    FANNY
M. de Narbonne?

M. D'ARBLAY

Bien.

FANNY

Ma Soeur?

M. D'ARBLAY

Bien, bien.

FANNY

Et Norbury–

M. D'ARBLAY

Et tous! Tous se portent bien!

And that's exactly the sort of conversation you can understand if you've had high school French. Basically, all she's doing is asking him how her sister is—and a bunch of other people they know—and that's like day one of high school French. It's pretty elementary stuff. But the letter about the cavalry scheme is way more advanced than that. It's not just in French—it's in *eighteenth-century* French—and it seems to involve a lot of conditional tenses, and the impoverished academics who make it their life's work to study Fanny don't even begin to translate it for you.

That seems kind of cruel, doesn't it?

You'd think they could help you out a little. But I

guess they assume that if you're actually attempting to read this stuff—well, then, surely you've been to graduate school and you can read French on your own, so they don't want to insult your intelligence by translating it for you.

Or possibly they're just being spiteful.

From what I hear, graduate school can be pretty rough. Worse than Hollywood, in fact. Competitive, star-driven, political. I was actually going to go at one point, so I could study up on Fanny in some sort of official capacity. Back when I was still in my twenties, going to grad school and getting a PhD in English seemed like a good idea to me—or at least it seemed like a *better* idea than crying in the stairwell at the alternative newspaper every Tuesday night for the rest of my life. So I took the GRE and sent away for applications, but then one Thursday night during a particularly good episode of *ER,* I got the Phone Call That Changed My Life. All in all, I'm pretty glad I answered that call. It was from this woman who used to be my boss at the New York Public Library when I was a struggling twenty-something assistant-girl, and she said, and I quote...

FAIRY-GODMOTHER-TYPE CHARACTER
I think you should move to LA
and work for my son, and he
should help you be a TV writer.

So I did.

I never went to graduate school. I never even finished filling out the applications—although you know who did go to graduate school?

Dave.

That's why he's so much older than the other assistants and why he's read so many books written before 1900. For the record, it's also why he wears those goddamn flip-flops all the time. I guess before he moved out here, he spent six long, hard, graduate school winters on the East Coast, and so the second he touched down in California, he made some kind of vow that he would never wear real shoes again unless he absolutely had to, which seems a little ridiculous to me, but then who am I to talk?

I've made a lot of ridiculous vows in my time.

Dave actually just sent me an email a little bit ago. Jill sent me one too—hours ago, wishing me good luck and all that—but Dave's didn't come till just now. He said everyone at the office was really sorry they weren't going to see me—and meet my little sister—but that of course they all understood about me not wanting to drive all the way to Burbank. He also said he'd miss emailing with me, but that obviously I should get this whole brain-surgery thing crossed off my list of things to do so we could go out and get drunk again real soon.

Although that's not really how I would characterize what happened.

Alcohol was definitely imbibed in a public place,

but it's not like we intentionally went out and got drunk. He came over to my place to fix my TiVo, and I offered him a beer while he was doing it because that seemed like the hospitable thing to do, and at some point we decided to go out and get some dinner at this place on La Brea, and then we got to talking—and drinking—and maybe I was a little drunk because just a few sips of any sort of pastel-colored fourteen-dollar drink and I'm pretty much a goner. But nothing happened.

I mean nothing untoward happened.

We just hung out and talked.

Like Fanny and Jeremiah Crutchley at Mrs. Thrale's summer house.

Like Fanny and George Owen Cambridge at the house on St. Martin's Street.

Like Fanny and Colonel Digby while the King was going mad.

That's all we did, just talked. And then he walked me to my car—which I was too cheap to valet park—and then I drove him to his car—which he was also too cheap to valet park—and then we said good night in the front seat of my Volkswagen Beetle convertible, and that was it.

Fade out.

Opportunity for romance over.

Obviously, this modern-day spinster story would have a much more stirring conclusion if we had gone back to my place and had sex, but being one of the Wishy-Washy, Dave didn't make any kind of pass at me, and what was I going to do? Make a pass at him? I mean, how would that even work exactly? How would a thirty-eight-year-old spinster seduce some other girl's boyfriend in the front seat of a Volkswagen Beetle convertible? The whole scenario sounds like ten tons of work to me—and also, you know, just not very nice.

After all, I'm sure Dave's girlfriend—*if I ever actually met her*—would probably end up being quite a bit like me. Definitely thinner and better-looking than I am, but she's basically my age, right? That fact has already been established, and based on Dave's reaction to the shoe contest, I think it's safe to say she doesn't own $40,000 worth of designer shoes.

Also, we've already established that she knows some of the same alternative-press-type people I know from back when I lived in Brooklyn, and nearly all the people I knew back then were quite a bit like me, and all the people *they* knew were a lot like them and so on and so forth—only none of us realized this at the time because it was the nineties and we were all super busy being alternative. Plus, I'm guessing she probably reads a lot of books written before 1900 because *Dave* reads a lot of books that were written before 1900, and while many people would find that annoying and affected, I can't exactly judge him for this behavior because I used to do the exact same thing back when I was a struggling twentysomething assistant. In fact, that's pretty much *all* I did back then: I read books written before 1900 and plotted out creative ways to give people my spec scripts without annoying them too much. That's why I couldn't really be too bummed when Dave gave me his, could I? Giving people your spec scripts is something you *have* to do if you're trying to get ahead in the entertainment industry. It's never pleasant. It's never fun. But—oh shit. I just realized something.

That's exactly what happens in the third act of *Hannah and Her Sisters*.

I never really thought about it this way before, but a spec script is actually what brings the lovers together at the end. A spec script and the dumb luck of running into each other at the Tower Records near Lincoln Center, which doesn't exist anymore.

But then again, neither do records.

It's crazy really, if you think about it, how much time has passed since they made *Hannah and Her Sisters*. When you watch it now, it seems like a period movie. You know, like some sort of bizarre, old-fashioned costume drama from a time before people had cell phones. I was still in high school when it came out, still living in the Rust Belt, and back then we didn't have Woody Allen movies in my town.

Or even in my state.

No, back then you had to drive all the way to Chicago if you wanted to see anything fancy or intellectual like that.

Oh, shoot. You know what just occurred to me?

Maybe I should stop Journaling for Anxiety™ and answer that email Dave sent me. Nothing he said really seemed to require a response, so probably I shouldn't, right? Let's face it, if I write back to him now, at this ridiculously late hour, it's going to look like I'm thinking about him in the middle of the night right before I'm about to have brain surgery.

Which I guess I am, when you get right down to it.

Jill thinks that means I'm actually in love with Dave. She slipped up and used that word the other day. She said it was because I talk about him all the time. But I talk about Fanny all the time, and I'm not in love with her.

I just like to think about her.

About her career struggles.

Her financial woes.

Her romantic difficulties.

About all the mistakes she made, the many things she got wrong over the course of her eighty-seven anxiety-ridden years on the planet—and about how everything still turned out okay for her in the end. The rudest, bitchiest, most judgmental of Fanny's biographers would say this was all luck. That's how she tells the story. She says that in January 1793, Fanny was aging and bitter and borderline neurotic and then—boom—she got really lucky and stumbled upon some love.

But we create our own luck, don't we?

I think I heard that once on *Oprah*. And Oprah

wouldn't say it if it weren't true. At the very least we have to be *prepared* for luck to find us. We have to lay the groundwork. To use an example from *Hannah and Her Sisters*, you can't just run into your older sister's ex-husband at Tower Records and ask him to read your spec script if you haven't actually *written* the spec script. That's why I, personally, think Fanny must have done something to deserve the happiness that came to her in the spring of 1793.

Of course, I still don't have any idea what it was.

If I figure it out, I'm definitely going to write that self-help book.

Arnie Greenblatt will be totally stoked if I do that, since self-help books about falling in love tend to sell really well. They basically just fly off the shelves.

Even the ones that are *not* mentioned on *Oprah*.

My best guess is that it must have something to do with hope. If you look closely, it's always lurking there in Fanny's diary, especially in the parts where the King is going mad. Like on Sunday, November 23, 1788, she describes Digby as being "of the despairing side" and reports that her own hopes "never wholly fail."

Or in January 1789, she writes to her bubbly, much-hotter little sister Charlotte…

> *We are all creatures of comparison and habit; every comparison here sinks me and my distress into nothing; and the force of habit is such that I now*

pass whole weeks in this gloom better than, ere thus
initiated, I could have passed a single day.

Even on December 22, 1788, when Digby took
leave of her for a week to spend Christmas with his
kids, and Fanny got stuck back at the palace playing piquet with the horrible Mrs. Schwellenberg—well, even
then she still had her birds, which makes her sound like
she's Cinderella or Saint Francis or something, but I
guess she used to leave food out for them, presumably
on her windowsill. So these little birds would come, no
matter how harsh the weather, to visit her in troops.
Hope is often portrayed that way, right? As a thing
with feathers? Well, back then, Fanny had hope. She
had it to spare and to share with others, and I think
that's what she did to deserve her happy ending.

And her very own six-part miniseries.

She hoped.

She persevered.

And no matter how bleak things got, she just kept
writing.

Her third chick-lit novel, *Camilla*, came out in
1796, and since she very smartly sold the copyright
and published it by subscription, it earned Fanny more
money than she had ever earned before. She and her
husband decided to spend it in a way that everyone
here in contemporary, twenty-first-century LA would
totally respect and appreciate: they built a house. A
cottage, technically. With two stories, four bedrooms,

and a skylight in the roof. So in the end, the young Miss Frances Burney, spinster, of the parish of St. Martin in the Fields, did wind up getting the real-estate-based happily-ever-after. But she got it in a distinctly twenty-first-century way: she earned it herself.

By her pen.

Which is also how I happen to own a first edition of that very same book. It's in five volumes, and at the front it has a list of more than a thousand people who agreed to pay a guinea for it, sight unseen, including a bunch of dukes and duchesses and one Miss J. Austen of Steventon. It also has *ſ*s where the letter *s* should be, so it's kind of difficult to read, and it cost—well, let me put it this way:

It cost two pairs of designer shoes.

But I feel like it was money well spent.

You know, to own a little piece of Fanny's life, a little piece of her happiness.

In March 1794, she wrote to her father describing her married life with M. D'Arblay as "tranquil, undisturbed and undisturbing."

Can life, he often says, be more innocent than ours, or happiness more inoffensive? He works in his garden, or studies English and mathematics, while I write. When I work at my needle, he reads to me; and we enjoy the beautiful country around us in long and romantic strolls, during which he carries

under his arm a portable garden-chair, lent us by
Mrs. Lock, that I may rest as I proceed.

That sounds kind of hokey, I know. "Long and romantic strolls"? So cliché, right? So exactly the kind of thing that tends to happen at the end of traditional, by-the-numbers Hollywood romantic comedies. I guess even if you try your hardest to tell an unconventional love story—one that breaks all the rules because the hero and heroine don't even meet until they're middle-aged and expired, and plus, hello, the female protagonist doesn't really give a shit about shoes—well, even then you just wind up fading out on something totally hokey like a long, romantic stroll. The detail about the garden-chair is kind of funny, but Fanny was never one of those super outdoorsy types, like Elizabeth Bennet who would walk for miles across muddy fields. Fanny was more of a city girl. And, of course, it's entirely possible that she was pregnant when she wrote that. On December 18, 1794, when she was forty-two years old, Frances Burney, Mother of English Fiction, gave birth to a son named Alexandre, after his father. She outlived him too, of course. But I don't have the heart to get into all that right now. I've got to go and have brain surgery, and for some reason this seems like a good place to stop…with two people in love and about to have a baby.

Dawn is breaking, and it follows all the rules.

ACKNOWLEDGMENTS

Thank you to Colleen Dunn Bates, Dorie Bailey, Caitlin Ek, Julianne Johnson, Katelyn Keating, and everyone at Prospect Park Books for taking a chance on *The Spinster Diaries*—but first and foremost to the intern who read it and loved it. Zoe LaDu, you're the best!

I was just about ready to put this book in a drawer and give up entirely when I found my literary agent, Gregory Messina. A huge thank you to him for believing in the book—and to Ben Hayes and Stephanie Barczewski for their part in helping me find Greg. Thanks also to my TV agents, Ari Greenburg and Zachary Druker at WME, for helping me stay gainfully employed while I was writing the book, to Amy Tierney for a great author photo, and to Laura Birek for website design.

I'm deeply grateful to have known the late George Hodgman. His thoughts on the book were astute and invaluable, and his generosity and sweetness inspired me to keep going. Thank you as well to my fellow students in George's 2016 Aspen Summer Words novel-editing workshop—Melissa Chadburn, Leah Worthy, Lynda Montgomery, Vinod Busjeet, and Eleanor Shelton—and to all the other passionate, dedicated, and talented writers I met at Aspen Summer Words and also at the Sirenland Writers Conference.

While *The Spinster Diaries* is technically a novel, Professor Catherine Parisian fact-checked the manuscript for me at an early stage. Thanks to her for lending me her Burney expertise.

Dana Greenblatt read this book more times than I can remember and never stopped asking me about it. Never. Ever. Even when I wanted her to. Same with Kimberly Dukes, who has been (foolishly) believing in me with all her heart and soul since I brought her that subway token in the fall of 1986. Adam Langer gave me early encouragement that I will be forever grateful for. Thanks to him and to everyone else who read the book along the way.

Gayle Abrams, Workplace Best Friend, vaulted into a whole new category when she invited me to go walking with her at Fryman circa 2000...and we have never stopped walking (at least metaphorically). And talking. And trying to find our voices as writers. Thank you, R.

Like Frances Burney, I owe a huge debt to my father, who passed away in 2010. What little money he made filling prescriptions and playing drugstore, he squandered on my fancy Ivy League education. I would not be where I am without him. Same is true of my mom and my siblings. A spinster novelist needs amazing nieces and nephews to fulfill the stereotype. Thanks to my brother and sisters, I have seven.

One final category: thanks for everything. To Danny Reichert, who is now REQUIRED to sit here with me. And to Anita Harrison, who never stopped listening.

About the Author

GINA FATTORE is a moderately successful television writer whose credits include *Dare Me*, *Better Things*, *Masters of Sex*, *Parenthood*, *Californication*, *Gilmore Girls*, and *Dawson's Creek*. Before moving to Los Angeles to become a TV writer, she was an assistant editor at the *Chicago Reader*. Her essays and reviews have appeared there and also in *The Millions*, *Salon*, and *McSweeney's Internet Tendency*. In 2015 she delivered a TEDx talk about spinsterhood called "Become What You Believe."